LEAVING

Also by Sergio Waisman

Literary Criticism

Borges and Translation: The Irreverence of the Periphery

Translations

The Absent City by Ricardo Piglia
Assumed Name by Ricardo Piglia
Dreams and Realities: Selected Fiction of Juana Manuela Gorriti
Juan de la Rosa: Memoirs of the Last Soldier of the Independence Movement by Nataniel Aguirre

Lesley!
Thank you for coming to my dear's seminar, and for your amazing book about the SOA. Hope you enjoy my little novel!
Sergio W.
11/06
DC

LEAVING

Sergio Waisman

Hurricane
An imprint of *InteliBooks* Publishers

Cover Design: Damion Gordon - BPT Graphx

Cover Illustration: *Untitled*, 64 x 49 cms., by Ecuadorian painter Manuel Rendón (1884-1982).

An earlier version of the section of Chapter 4 found on pages 109-115 first appeared as "The Watchmaker's Son" in *Glimmer Train 39* (Summer 2001).

ISBN 0-932367-11-9

This book was printed in the United States of America
To order additional copies of this book, contact:

InteliBooks
www.intelibooks.com
orders@intelibooks.com

For Maureen & Emma

CONTENTS

El original es infiel a la traducción
[The original is unfaithful to the translation]
—Jorge Luis Borges

BEGINNING WITH TODAY

Stuck again, I want to speak of piano staircases, accordion halls, of long walks in salty breezes, searching for reason in a madwoman's soliloquy. Of large mirrors blank as I stand before them.

The beginning, in this context, a question. Not unlike what we allow ourselves. As opposed to what is imposed upon us, the laws of nature. Is the randomness that brought us together in a café in the Mission district the same which ulcerated several feet of my large intestine a few years ago? Is that what we should call it, random?

Wait a moment, I'd like to try again. Today, in the middle of February, it is 60° F. Everything is upside down. Until yesterday there was snow on the ground and it was dropping to below 20° at night. What has happened to our winter? Last week I shoveled the sidewalk and salted the wooden steps outside our front door, and now the sun shines bright and warm? I see people outside: some in shorts, others biking to school or work. Around noon, four gray heads jog in a tight group, healthy middle-aged men exercising for lunch.

I open several windows in our apartment to let fresh air in for the first time in weeks. This morning we talked about a blue guitarist who crossed the Atlantic to witness silver lands and breathe, just breathe. Now, I brew a pot of strong coffee, serve myself a large piece of chocolate hazelnut cake and take a seat at the kitchen table.

Suddenly it is hot and the wind coming in through the open window in the kitchen—the one facing southeast—feels like it is coming from the sea. The sea, in Colorado? But no, it is not the sea, not exactly. Not completely the marine feel of ocean winds. What could it be, then? A wind that has swept above open waters, wide enough to resemble the sea. And there is something else in the air, too; but there are no oceans or even large lakes near us. What could this unexpected warmth blowing in through my Boulder window be? Could it… Yes, I recognize it now. I can even see it, for there is a silvery haze to it. It is the ocean-like breeze off the port of the Río de la Plata mixing with the smoke of the Sunday *asados* drifting over the pampas. This breeze, in turn, reminds me of the bitter herb of *mate* in a hand-held gourd. And of the sounds of Spanish interspersed with Yiddish around another kitchen table, very far from this one, in an inner patio in Buenos Aires.

Inside, this breeze and the surprising sensations it triggers is warm through and through, almost moist. I remain sitting like this for a long while, my eyes closed and yet a part of me still seeing, as if my senses could reach down all the way across the globe to the Southern Hemisphere, back against the steady current of time, and somehow absorb the past through outstretched fingers, through my very skin, up and out of the basket we call memory. It is my body that is reaching against the currents, down, back. Voices and faces from the past rush in all at once, surround me on all sides. The house in the dream and the many houses left behind by families moving on to better lives. Walking through a city that is—and is not—my hometown. Chasing a soccer ball in a square after school, gathering rubber plant leaves for a boy's private collection. Falling in love with songs of swallows flying through colonial arches, their shadows tracing our stories on adobe walls. Patterns that suggest new ways to draw up maps.

Eventually, I start cooling off. I don't know how long I have been sitting in my kitchen. Involuntarily, I open my eyes; it is darker out and there is no trace of the sudden heat that just a moment ago entered the apartment. It is considerably colder now, much too cold to just sit here, and I must get up to close the windows. As I do so, I notice that there is still plenty of snow up in the mountains, as well as on the field across from our building, and that the sun has already begun to go down. I was wrong earlier about the change of seasons; we are still very much in the thick of winter. It is later in the day than I had thought, and you should be getting home soon.

I go back to my grandparents' shop in the Bronx, find myself sifting through strings, clothing and buttons. Playing with pins, pincushions and thimbles in the rear room while my grandmother measures alterations on customers out front. I trace my need for a beginning there, sitting at my grandfather's feet: a framework of light and texture, sounds and smells. As always, he works stooped over the material, sewing silently, deliberately. On the shelf above the old Singer a radio tuned to a Spanish station plays mostly loud commercials, some *boleros*. The air is singed and musty, an iron heating the moisture. My grandmother's hairspray and the strange orange-like smell of the pomade my grandfather uses to keep his hair in place. My grandmother, who has learned a fair amount of English, is the one who deals with the customers; my grandfather never goes up front. Although he was to live in New York City for fourteen years—speaking Yiddish with his friends and broken Spanish with the Puerto Ricans in their neighborhood—he never got past hello in English.

And you trace it *there,* you ask, where your grandparents watched over you while your parents were at work? As if it all had to do with a tailor from Lublin via Buenos Aires. As if it could be narrowed down to a few words and strings, just like that. An early memory away from home. A name, a place, an image. Needles threaded, seams sewn in a crowded shop in the Bronx, a patchwork of cloth joined by a grandfather's hands into elegant suits and dresses. For perhaps it can serve as a point of departure: from a time before memory to a time where memory became all there was to distinguish myself from the world around me.

The blue-striped bands framing the yellow sun on the white middle of the Argentine flag rose every morning, assisted by the high-pitched voices of the students at Sarmiento Elementary School. We lined up in our respective grades in the school's inner courtyard at 8:00 A.M., the teachers at the head of each class, then the students, from shortest to tallest in height. In front of us our teachers, above the flag and the sky and behind the ancient rubber tree around which we based all our games: at times, pretending that its large leafs were *pesos*, we traded them secretly in class; at others, we chased one another in circles, slapping each other with the same leafs, the thick sinewy trunk of the tree serving as a safe haven where you could not get hit. Some even collected these leafs as their own rare coins or stamps and snuck them into their bags when no one was watching. Future bookmarks for books yet unwritten.

The teachers shouted to get us under control; a stillness eventually settled over the courtyard, as we finally stopped fidgeting and talking and teasing and fell quietly and dutifully into our places in line. The hushed silence only lasted a brief moment before the singing of the national anthem began; and yet, as brief as it was, I remember it to this date: a gasp before a fall. It was so ephemeral that a stranger, had he not known that it occurred every day at the same time of morning, would have easily missed it. It was the only silence that the school's courtyard ever witnessed. At all other times the courtyard was filled with splashing laughter and screams, cascades of teasing words, currents of the shouts and games of the boys and girls. Even when the courtyard was empty— when everyone was in their classrooms, or at night, or on the weekends—it was never truly silent, for the echo of the children's voices was trapped inside by the brick walls and was constantly stirred by the wind—much like the whirlwind that spun the rubber tree leafs around the base of the tree. But for that instant, before the crackle and static of the loudspeakers broke the stillness in the air, even the echoes were extinguished and the silence held us rigid and motionless, forcefully pulling our undivided attention to the base of the mast, where the flag would soon rise, accompanied by the soft singing of our small individual voices.

The anthem began and the flag rose up the pole. Being average in height, I always fell somewhere in the middle of my class for the four years I attended school there: safe in anonymity, for a while, in the middle of a perfectly straight line from shortest to tallest. A gasp before a fall. The last words of the anthem—*Oíd, mortales, el grito sagrado: Libertad, libertad, libertad*—hung in the crisp air as we looked up from our places in line. Singing clearly and loudly and together now so as to sound better than the raspy recording from the loudspeaker in the corner of the courtyard opposite the flag mast.

My parents lived at home until they married. My father Eduardo shared a room with his brother Norberto in a cramped apartment in Villa Crespo, his two sisters Margarita and Celina in an even smaller room across the hallway. He would leave home as early in the day as possible, even at the age of eleven or twelve, and go to work with his father to repair watches—or sometimes instead of his father, who would take a detour around the corner to the café to play dice for hours on end—and then attend the afternoon sessions of school.

Villa Crespo, as little Edu headed out the door every morning, was (as my father himself has told me) the drifting chords of the song of the Italian bricklayers, the hammering from the "La Joven Cataluña" garage, a group of *señoras* crowing over the merchandise with the fruit vendor Alí, an eighteen-year-old girl singing the words to "El Pañuelito" as she cleaned the sidewalk with exaggerated sweeps of the broom, the grandiloquent offers of the Jewish cloth merchants, and the clamoring of kids kicking a stuffed sock down the street.

My mother Ester, meanwhile, lived in Chacarita, the next neighborhood over, with her older brother Carlos and younger sister Diana, in a dark house with water stains on the walls and a cold inner patio that led to her parents' bedroom with its thick orange bedspread and the black and white television set on one side, and to a small kitchen and bathroom on the other. There was a large cemetery located conveniently nearby—as my mother's Bube liked to say from her perch on the kitchen stool, as if to assure a constant sense of gloom—and, three blocks down, a circular plaza built in 1910, Parque Centenario, around which cars sped at all hours of the day and night.

My mother speaks about the *mate* that she drank as a child with her aunts in their patio, the Yiddish she learned and knew well at one point, the *shul* she avoided and the *shule* she attended, the meetings she was allowed to hold in the living room when she was a teenager, and a special gathering, once—in that same small house where she lived until she married my father at the age of twenty—that included a visit from La Negra, before she had recorded her first album.

* * *

I, for my part, since moving away from San Diego to college, have lived in five cities, encompassing eleven apartments and eighteen roommates. In this, at least, you and I are not so different. Three states ago, we moved in together. And perhaps it is because the rest is not history, to go against the saying, that this search for a beginning has begun. Last summer, we hauled 6,500 pounds west on I-80 from Providence to Boulder. I drove the U-haul with our books and clothes and the old furniture that we have accumulated from various garage sales in the truck, pulling our '88 Honda Civic behind us. That car was our first purchase together—appropriately an automobile, as you like to say, to mark the American nature of our travels. We brought a cooler with sandwiches and canned ice tea up front to keep us going, plus a small cactus that has survived all of our moves. Most stops—out of New England, through the industrial northeast, across the Midwest and into the high plains—were for me to run into a bathroom. The U-haul with the Civic attached behind was extremely difficult to maneuver, so I never backed up, drove the entire distance heading forward. Now, looking west again to our next move, we continue to head back: a partial return, even if we know there is no such thing. Convenience, you say, is much more than choosing a life style.

It is the continuity of the kitchen table, its function as a constant, which draws me to it. Not to mention what is certain to be on it: a strong cup of coffee, morning or night. It is here that we alternate clipping coupons, planning meals, transforming days into lists. I want to remember the imagined, and imagine memory. Be able to trace footsteps that left Poland, found Argentina, only to leave again. I believe there is a line between imagination and reality which can be made to fade. And, simultaneously, in the space that remains, a different kind of line will emerge: a genealogy seen and heard through language. *Skuhtzl kumt*—well, look who's here!—as my Bube Cata says when someone walks through the door. I hope you are not out to circumvent time, you warn with a guilty smile. You have your lines too, I realize, as when you enter a world where turn-of-the-century women debate suffrage, mining towns engage syndicalism and migratory workers are seen pulling heads of lettuce in irrigated Central Valley fields from Highway 101 in California. But that's where the analogies end. For I will be traced by the figure of a tailor in Lublin and the daily activities of a watchmaker in Buenos Aires. You, raised by a high school teacher near a Franciscan Mission, were able to let the swallows and the picket lines come to you. Whereas I find myself time and time again at the same kitchen table, drinking this same strong coffee, looking out the window and not recognizing where I am. I search for beginnings because I do not remember. Can memory really tell you who you are, you ask, reminding me that it is not so simple, after all. Or the dead relatives I continue to imagine. I know, it's a big *ka-shuh*, no matter how you mix it up. I promise not to go as far back as the Old Testament, everything else is fair game.

When I was five years old I spoke fluent French—or so the story goes. I learned it in preschool in Orsay, near the lab where my father worked for a year on a post-doc. Then, just as easily as I had learned it, I forgot my French when we returned to Argentina, early in 1973. My sister, being too young for preschool, did not learn French as I did. Often we went out in the afternoons, walking in the shade of the Orsay neighborhood where our apartment was located, hand in hand. Stay with your brother, my mother always said, allowing me to play at being much older than I was. I developed the habit, whenever we were in a store or running errands somewhere, of asking for a piece of candy for my sister. *¿Un bonbon pour ma petite soeur, s'il vous plait?* was the line I used. My parents say that it worked every time.

A few cousins of mine still remember the French accent I had when we moved back to Buenos Aires. The story was already a favorite of theirs before we left Argentina in 1976, and they tell it over and over again when we are finally able to visit in 1983. After the first hot summer months trying to learn stickball, after a year in the middle of a perfect corn field, after a cross-country drive with a jar of crickets, from where we lived now in a house with a den and a backyard in San Diego, 1983. My grandparents organize a family gathering so everyone can see us and that is where the retelling—this retelling—begins. Claudio, Daniel and Josesito, in alternating fashion, recount how they rode with me on the back of the *colectivos* when we first moved back from France, how I'd look out the window and make comments about the streets or the people I had not seen in over a year, and how everything I said came out with a French accent, with rolling rr's and nasal vowels, so funny coming from the mouth of a curly-haired five-year-old *petisito*, trying to be all *canchero* but sounding more French than Napoleón, *carajo*, my mother's cousins say, as they take turns trying to imitate what I sounded like back then. And every time the *colectivero* slammed on the breaks, *este pibe grita ¡Merde!* and spits under his breath, they say and laugh, and I laugh too, although when they tell it it sounds like someone else altogether and not me sitting towards the back of the *colectivo* with them (*¿el 24? ¿el 60?*), rolling through Buenos Aires with a thorough confusion of tongues in my mouth, I really have no idea what they are talking about.

¿Un bonbon pour ma petite sœur, s'il vous plait? Par un décret des puissances suprêmes..., épouvantée et pleine de blasphèmes....

* * *

That year in France my father taught us to spit and say *¡Merde!* whenever we crossed a border. For good luck, he said. We were in the car when he explained it, about to enter Spain on a camping trip. You sit up, he said, look around, take in as much as possible, try to determine the point of crossing and right then and there you spit and shout—*¡Merde!*

I remember the dark green hills and the enormous smooth water-worn boulders and a few cluttered trees in the distance and not long after a stationary cow or two, the one-lane road and then the small house with the picture-book A-frame roof and the thin gate and the two flags and the man stepping out of the small house towards us with a gray beret and a long pointy bayonet—also right out of a picture book—and the man's olive eyes as he examines our passports and the smell of ham and coffee when he sticks his head briefly into our car and looks around before waiving us on.

My sister and I decided that this was immediately prior to crossing the border, although we were already sitting up and ready to spit. We giggled after we left the man in front of the small house, looked around again, saw the line that would bring us into Spain and as our Citröen rolled slowly across we did it, we spit towards each other and tried to duck, and both got sprayed, and all of us in the car, my parents as well as my sister and I, yelled *¡Merde!* as loud as possible in hilarious discordance. And that, my father said, is how you mark a moment of leaving.

Standing in a frozen field in Colorado, looking at a group of dairy cows. Each one with its distinct black and white pattern, chewing slowly, deliberately, as if daydreaming. Their rounded ears are dotted with burrs, as are their tails, swatting at invisible flies, some variety immune to this kind of weather. Your wool hat and scarf, the neck of your thick winter coat pulled all the way up and your hands buried deep in your pockets betray your California upbringing. I'm not nearly as cold for some reason, although I don't know at what point, at what age or longitude, my body became accustomed to these sub-freezing temperatures. I've certainly never been here before. It's not easy for you and me to exchange places, is it? you ask. For starters, I always need to know when things began. Or where, at least. It is easier to find the middle, however, a turn at which the end seems closer than the beginning. Although we know there is more than one of each of these. For example, our parents' mortality awakens our own. Your father's triple bypass surgery, already two years ago, is present now and always will be. We had thought that this could be a beginning: a college town at the foot of the Rocky Mountains, your new editorial position. But as soon as we arrived we began to miss New England (a safe feeling, you pointed out, since we knew we were not going back there) and I started on my applications for California. All this talk about a return to the Bay Area is starting to sound like it's our lost garden, you say. Our boots against the hard earth, the wind that tells us to go home as it rustles the weeds and the bushes, the chill creeping under our layered clothing. How comical they seem, the cows in this field, left alone here to chew slowly, at their leisure, with no one to milk them. Their expressions almost thoughtful.

A five-year-old in the Luxembourg Gardens, I'm leaning over the edge of a large fountain of water, pushing a little wooden boat out towards the center of the pool. The fountain is surrounded by other children, most a little older than me, also leaning over, looking after their ships. Behind them, concentrically, other children wait their turn, some of the bigger ones trying to maneuver their way in by pushing and shoving. Circling on the outer sphere of it all is a tall uniformed man with a deadly long stick, occasionally bending over the children on the ground, reaching far into the air space above the water, angling the stick down to redirect one of the boats back towards the edge, not letting them get too far from the sides of the fountain. The vessels cruise in those rough waters (on this day the wind is particularly strong and the man with the stick only seems to be agitating the water further) away from the quayside where the children release them to the mercy of the elements, risking collision with other ships, trying to navigate all the way to the small area in the center beyond the reach of the guard's stick.

Bent far over the side, my arms submerged up to my elbows in the cold water, I make waves with my hands under the surface to create more turbulence so my boat will sail free of the man's reach. (Even though my vessel is only a simple wooden dinghy, and it looks meager compared to most of the others—some with small triangular sails, others with even more intricate designs, everything from catamarans to speed racing boats to navy destroyers—I know it is sturdy, and quick.) I wish so hard that it would float away from the children beside and behind me, that it would go free of the finely trimmed lawns, the manicured gardens and the geometrically perfect paths around the fountain from which one must absolutely not stray (or else one is reprimanded by a loud whistle from an angry *gendarme* and the shaking heads of all the adults who happen to witness the impropriety of the misbehaved little boy)—I am urging my boat so hard and I can feel my heart pumping inside my chest. Hoping it might somehow achieve the center, the space where, if the weather holds, it could float in total abandon, beyond anyone's reach or command, if even for a brief moment or two.

But it is not meant to be. A smart smack of the long stick on the water's surface in front of me breaks my expectations instantly. *¡Ne fait pas ça! ¡Quité tes bras de l'eaux!* the tall thin man in the blue uniform yells in a squeaky loud voice, looking straight down at me from above. All I can see of his face when I look up is his sharp chin and nose; the rest is shaded by his official cap. I take my arms out of the water—guilty, caught. My wet arms, suddenly out of the water, make me feel very cold and my whole body trembles. The man redirects my dinghy back to me (how does he always know which one belongs to which child?); I grab it and quickly give up my place at the fountain's edge to a bigger kid who has been anxiously waiting behind me, breathing loudly into my neck for some time now.

The university only seems to accentuate the split, an ineluctable fragmentation of tongues and voices. All the years it will take to complete this degree—from Cide Hamete to Pierre Menard, from Quentin Compson to Emilio Renzi— will not take me back to another life, un-lived. It will not rid me of English. It will not undo migration. San Diego welcomed me, said forget Argentina—you are here now. Just like Buenos Aires had welcomed my grandparents, said forget Poland—you are on the shores of the Río de la Plata now. Years disappeared, an adolescence lost. A new address, a road not taken, conflicting loyalties. On the soccer field, in the plaza, in the South Atlantic.

The first few years in San Diego was countless afternoons listening to Padres games after school. Picturing the difference between a curve and a slider from the intonation of an announcer's voice. A pop-up from a deep fly by the thud of the bat crack heard through the portable radio resting against the steps by the front door. Crouched in the driveway, bouncing a tennis ball off the garage door, fielding it in webbed leather. Retraining muscles under the California sun. Far from a gray square in Belgrano lined with old people chatting on wooden benches, dogs chasing children chasing a soccer ball after school, juggling, heading and shooting it around the statue of Alberdi sitting in the center of a boy's world.

I did not come to this decision on my own. Moving, traveling, raising questions about language. This, a desire to name beginnings. Driving to Newport in our beige Civic soon after purchasing it. Your hands on the steering wheel, your profile against the moving scenery, curves of an outline I can see with eyes opened or closed. Who brought it up first, I do not remember even that. My first outing after a nine-month colitis flare-up. The translating—that part of the plan, at least—came naturally. Then again, you have been a translator your whole life, you said. New England was waves of dark green along Highway 95, a hint of colors changing, drawn beyond your perfect silhouette. Nature in motion. You helped me complete the picture. By the time we crossed the Jamestown Bridge, we had traced ourselves a new map, compiled a list of cities you and I would live in, and then leave behind.

Does it get me any closer, I wonder. This, changing tenses, shifting focus, mixing memories with projections. Pouring desire into words that travel from me to you and back again. The thought of me in your hands, the soft touch of your fingers, a gaze that asks who is leading whom. Muted voices finally emerge, demand an utterance, confuse a look ahead with a search for an origin. Ghosts materialize, snow melts, rivers flow. Until solitude springs up again, with or without words, takes shape, invades our everyday.

When I was ten years old and we arrived in New York from Buenos Aires, before moving on to Illinois for a year and then to San Diego, my father told my sister and me that, with time, we would learn to pronounce better than he all those strange English words that sounded like blah blah blah with potatoes in your mouth and made us laugh so hard. We did not believe him. It was more fun to say ¡*Merde*! and spit as far as we could see. Blah blah blah we repeated over and over again, pretending we knew it all. Laughing and spitting. ¡*Merde*!

Time passes. For once the change in language sinks in, my name changes on your lips and so do I. With the years, with you. I have come to like your mispronunciation—the American pronunciation, I should say. And mine too now. You make it easier to be both, to see the forces that drive the split as a beginning instead of an end.

(You have a queer name, Sergio.)

We started talking about children and a family and wanting to live closer to our parents. In our sweats, a slow Sunday morning with the New York Times on the kitchen table in Rhode Island. Providence. Breakfast was thick cuts of egged-bread, as you called it, a pot of coffee and the small beads of perspiration on the small of your back after sex. Should we get married, one of us asked. I do not remember who did the asking. We had not brushed our teeth yet. No trumpeters before a vice-royal audience, no bells tolling from Saxon towers, no jesters dancing down narrow cobblestoned streets, no champagne fizzling in crystals raised to glowing chandeliers, no silver flares sparkling into a broad river, no verses dating back to Provençal bards—and yet, outside, the wind rustled through the leafs of the elm in front of our apartment, a green so green we could feel it inside. And the wind, wanting to stay there, spinning wide leafs in their own shade, transformed the tree from a still life into a living being, full of breath. A translation. Showing us, for a moment. The movements of a present to remember.

Everyday I read more Spanish than ever before. Write papers, attend seminars, teach. All in the language of my childhood. Another beginning. One that will loop around, in part, take me back to earlier ones, perhaps. But it will also reveal the split. Tongues and voices, a constant concern for words. You and I. I have been here too long, and I know I will never be all of who I am. The closest I ever come is sitting back, naming ghosts, with you. And you are in English.

My aunt Diana was born in 1950, when her sister (my mother) Ester was twelve years old. Soon afterwards, their family became one of the first in the neighborhood to get a television. It was small, black and white, and they promptly set it up in the parents' bedroom. The parents, my Zeide Pedro and my Bube Cata, moved Diana's crib out of their room to make space for the television, which, they have always claimed, accelerated when Diana learned to walk. At seven months, she climbed out of her crib in her sister's room and crawled back to her parents' room, where the family was gathered in front of the new set. A month later she was walking. She grew up in that dark room, whose only window faced the cold patio, climbing on and off the tall spongy bed with the thick orange bedspread, the TV always on. By the time she was fourteen months old, she was sitting on the edge of the large soft bed, her sister on one side and her father on the other, watching Perón's speeches, broadcast during the presidential campaign of 1951. The cameras picked up the chanting and cheering of the populous crowds wherever he went, from Córdoba to Jujuy, from Entre Ríos to Mendoza. Then, as the camera zoomed in, the General would appear, his face solemn (perhaps already in anticipation of Evita's death), and everyone would grow silent. His speeches were short but lively; as my mother explains it, you were proud to live in Argentina when you heard him speak. Pedro, watching and listening, taking a break from his measuring and stitching, was reminded of the discussions in which he participated in when he first arrived in Buenos Aires, when Jews from Eastern Europe debated whether to follow Zionism or other kinds of Socialism, before the War, before options became limited. I can imagine my mother, Ester, watching quietly, thinking of what her friends and her teacher would have to say about that night's speech the next day in school, already absorbing the words she would later take with her to the Youth Group meetings and the pages of the *Juventud* magazine. Eventually the impassioned speech would come to an end, the crowds in the provinces would go wild, and Diana—still in diapers, her mouth half full of baby teeth, her round eyes brown and wide, bouncing on the edge of the bed—would throw up both her small arms, her tiny fingers held in the V for victory position, and scream out, along with the rest of his followers on the television set, *Perón, Perón*—the first word she learned after *mamá*.

* * *

In the elections of November 1951, the first under the new constitution, Perón swept into a second term as president. Following the introduction of female suffrage, the Peronist vote grew from 1.4 million, or 54%, in 1946 to 4.6 million, or 64%, five years later. His *Justicialista* party won majorities in each of the provinces and the capital and carried every seat in the Senate.

Perón began his second six-year term in June 1952, but he endured scarcely three more years, until the so-called *Revolución Libertadora* of September 1955.

On July 26, 1952, at 8:25 pm, Eva Perón died of cancer, after the country observed her slow decline for months. *Es el triste deber de la Secretaría de Prensa y Difusión de la Presidencia, de informar al pueblo argentino que, Eva Perón, jefa espiritual de la Nación, entró en la inmortalidad a las 20 y 25 del día de hoy.* She was thirty-three years old.

The premise is simple: I believe in a world in which spelling is phonetic. And then there's the rest. Universities as the only landmarks: Illinois, California, Rhode Island, Colorado. A collection of bookmarks beginning with the leafs of a rubber tree plant. Place has lost meaning, only scratched albums and the irreverence of translation remain to give evidence. The Equator as the looking glass, displacement as the recurrent theme. A ghost speaking about other ghosts, as if the link that usually binds things together had been cut. Because I need that familiar accent, the informal second person conjugation. The streets they walked in Villa Crespo, Chacarita, the cafés where they flocked to get away from their parents. A song that is not mine. I was not there. And yet, the slant of the words, the self-assured intonation, is as electricity in me. Music is like that, you say, it's everyone's, even when tongues travel. A life lived here, not there. But I insist, to your occasional dismay, that the life not lived does exist—ghost or no ghost. What formula, what hypothesis or theoretical principle can account for this?

Imagine a place where husband and wife are both satisfied every time, where colons function as they should. Where meetings in bars are not interrupted by possibilities unrealized, or relegated to an imaginary south. Or better yet, the family stays, the father of the ghost forgets politics, exchanges one abstraction for another, chooses physics over Peronism (over the crazy Peronism of the youth of the early 70s). Different models, different time lines. Better not, you begin to say. After all, so many left, so many disappeared, who's to say how far or near the dogs' snapping jaws really came? I'm afraid you will not find it there, you add, a dictionary on your lap, tracing definitions with your fingertip.

For ghost connotes the soul or spirit of life in death, but that's not what you mean, is it? Only in part. (*It was all in scraps and fragments.*) Any apparition, really, but more than that, in or between languages, the process of the projection, the echo of the motion. Distinct from the physical, but never free of it. Our bodies are here, even if love exists only in the words. A trace, a melody, a footprint. The wake in the atmosphere behind an airplane at 33,000 feet. Adding and subtracting hours to compensate for the circumference of Orbis Tertius. A conversation that seeks to defy time. As if we had never left. Almost, almost.

Instead, we embrace lives lived in reflected continents, hemispheres that shift with the blink of an eye, phone calls in the middle of the night for years to come. Memories, the substance upon which we persist, with you now, and texts that end with yes.

A man walks past in the narrow night, the cobblestone sound of Italian heels clicking near the plaza. Listen to the blue guitar, listen with your whole body. And the occasional barking of the neighborhood dogs. A city of mutts and small cats, as you will say one day. I remember a madwoman dancing waltzes in her head, a great-aunt baking in a kitchen hotter than the oven, *pretzelech* and *mate* for a *merienda* in a covered patio of an empty house.

A coworker at the library talks about book collecting, the importance of first editions, of a typo even. On a dark New England freeway we drove with my parents, on the weekend that they came to visit us during our year in Providence, as they sang along to Mercedes Sosa. I could think of nothing as I stared at the black pavement unrolling before me.

I have a distinct memory of watching a cartoon version of *Gulliver's Travels* on our black and white television in the living room of our two-bedroom apartment in Orsay, France. I don't remember speaking French, and I can't picture myself saying anything in French other than *¿Un bonbon pour ma petite soeur, s'il vous plait?*, but I know I understood *Gulliver's Travels*, for I remember minute details of the plot and of the cartoon characters and their land and seascapes. Today I reread the four voyages filtered through the memory of a French animated translation. The image of a part-time giant/part-time midget sailing from Lilliput to Brobdingnag is my proof that I know French, that I spoke French at some stage in my life, as a five-year old, which, in any case, I promptly forgot at my next port of entry: kindergarten in Belgrano. My story since then (both before and after) has meant to say the thing which was not. (Before: from Lublin to Buenos Aires; then: from Villa Crespo to the Bronx to Orsay and back; later: from Buenos Aires to New York in an unprecedented rush, on to Champaign-Urbana, from there to suburban San Diego; later still, after you and I fly east to Providence, this returning west and west to Boulder, and on to the Bay Area one day.)

I have tried to clear up the memory, but it only becomes more equivocal with time, as if I were digging down instead of up and still expected to come out into some kind of light. Children are a wonder at that age, my father says on one occasion when I bring up the topic at dinner, the way they pick up languages, but then he grows suddenly uncharacteristically quiet, reminiscing, perhaps, about that year in France and everything that followed upon our return to Argentina. As if languages were crumbs dropped by others along invisible paths, my father seems to be saying. But you and I and other children in motion may disagree. Blind burrows and the growth of rhizomes, we will want to add. Talking again, as if he were an anthropologist instead of a physicist, my father speaks of traveling tribes who rely on their young to learn the tongues of the new land through local games. Thus, he concludes, they swiftly make it their own, adapt themselves to it and vice versa, that's how they manage. Spanish, English, Yiddish, French, it doesn't matter which, children are like a giant ear in the dark, absorbing every sound for miles around.

After leaving my parents at the hotel, alone again, you and I revisit the topic at the kitchen table. There is no property in language, you say as you stir your coffee, your father is right but he is also wrong. A child is of a tongue but he also makes a tongue his own. The cups, spoons and saucers, the sugar bowl and little pitcher of milk, the entire set on the table. Even Houyhnhnm is simple for children, simple in its infinite complexity, the perfection of naming to identify, but also naming for the sake of the sounds of the names, and the game between the two. Everything of and in the body, the entire body and the tongue united before separation, mirror or no mirror. Still stirring long after the sugar has dissolved. It is the conversation itself that matters, that is what my father does not understand even as he practices it, not the rejection of the accent but its beautiful texture, its form, the ingredients and the ingredients in the meal, apart and together. Yes, the inclusion of countless ports of exit and entry, *aduanas* and their checkpoints and officials with loaded weapons. Beautiful only when one has passed, or even if one has passed? That is our question, our leaving, yes.

La física del viejo

Plaza de Mayo was packed tight. My father lifted me above a sea of heads, sat me on his shoulders: October 1, 1973. We were there to hear Perón's first speech since his return to Argentina. It was what I had always imagined the *tribunas populares*—the standing-room-only sections of the stadium behind the goalies where the die-hard fans went—would be like, but where I was not allowed to go because I was too young. Men hung from the trees lining the plaza and all the avenues leading in were closed off to traffic and extended back for blocks-on-end with wall-to-wall humans. The deciduous trees had dropped their leaves and sprouted cheering young men instead. As we awaited Perón's appearance, my mother taught me some of the words that everyone was singing: *Los muchachos peronistas / todos unidos triunfaremos / y como siempre daremos / un grito de corazón / ¡Viva Perón! ¡Viva Perón!* The trees swayed as the men held on with one hand and waved with the other.

The last time that the Plaza had seen so many people was in September of 1955, when another multitude came out to celebrate, on that occasion, Perón's ouster. That particular event was marked a few days earlier by an aerial bombardment executed by naval planes that killed several dozen civilians shortly after dawn, burned most of the automobiles circling the Plaza as the city was beginning to awake, and left scars—still visible today—on the marble slabs of the buildings near the House of Government, including on the front of the Banco Nacional. History demonstrated then that the Plaza de Mayo was not exclusively Peronist; but at my first demonstration, it had been retaken.

My parents had brought me there, they wanted me to be a part of all this. I could not imagine a luckier seven-year old in the world, nor a better feeling than singing along with the hundreds of thousands who had come out to the center of the capital—to the center of the country—that day. I wanted to take it all in, not to miss anything. It was so crowded I could not see the ground. Men and women strained to get a better view of the Casa Rosada by jumping or standing on the balls of their feet. Their expressions were intense, their faces about to burst, and they looked familiar and all somehow alike, with wide eyes, mouths opening and closing, skin flush with excitement, bulky noses and strands of hair wet with sweat sticking to their foreheads. The mass number of people was overwhelming.

I looked up to escape the dizziness beginning to overtake take me. The few clouds in the blue above drifted like sailboats on a forgotten sea. I turned to the hundreds of flags hanging from the buildings flanking the plaza: blue and white along with innumerable signs and posters on every balcony as far as the eye could see. I wondered how they had mounted them all; in some cases they were hung from the windows of the banks on the retreating sides of Diagonal Norte (Av. Roque Sáenz Peña) and Diagonal Sur (Av. Julio A. Roca). But others were simply suspended, as if by magic—on the sides of the Cathedral, for example. And immediately above the crowd there were large banners that flowed like waves as the people holding their ends jumped up and down. These signs, with their curious symbols and mysterious acronyms, were elevated everywhere above the crowds pouring into the Plaza from the eleven streets that lead into it: down the width of the two Diagonales, from the Avenidas 25 de Mayo and Balcarce on either side of the Casa Rosada, from Reconquista, San Martín, and Rivadavia on the side of the Cathedral, from Defensa, Bolívar, and Hipólito Yrigoyen on the southern side of the Plaza, and down Av. de Mayo, the main tributary extending back behind us for fourteen blocks all the way to

Plaza de los dos Congresos, where I could see—as if it were a floating palace in some Oriental fairy tale—the dome of the nineteenth-century House of Legislature.

I tried to read the banners more carefully, but found that I could not decipher what they said. Again I thought of a stadium and of the signs that celebrate favorite players in the stands, or advertise coca cola and adidas on the banks around the field. I leaned down and asked my father what the signs meant. He said that people brought them to identify where they were from, to let everyone know that they were there, present on that day (JP, JUP, JTP, AE, etc.). As he spoke he pointed to the different banners, including some of the larger ones making their way down the streets to the right (CGT, SMATA, UOM, UTA, etc.). I listened, letting my eyes rest on the Cabildo—the most Colonial of the buildings surrounding the Plaza, between the corner of Diagonal Norte and Rivadavia and Av. de Mayo—and I recalled the field trip that I had taken with my elementary school class and the tour of the arches and the cool shaded patio and a brief history lesson about the representatives from the provinces who had come together over 150 years ago to try to invent a nation.

Although it was incredibly loud, I could hear my father clearly above the clamor and the uproar, as if his speech was on a different frequency than all the other voices. As he continued to identify the different groups present in the Plaza, the people around us—who had looked indistinguishable to me before, all somehow similar to one another—began to separate and individualize, as if they too were being delineated by his words. Then, suddenly, I remembered a geography lesson that we'd had earlier that school year. I remembered the afternoon that my teacher had stood at the front of the classroom before the elongated map of the southern cone of the Americas and traced the borders of Argentina, naming the provinces and the major natural formations and waterways, from Tierra del Fuego and the Patagonia, up the edge of the Cordillera shared with Chile, past Mendoza, San Juan and La Rioja, into Salta and Jujuy (*la botita*), barely above the Tropic of Capricorn; then the pointed finger turning east, around Tucumán and Santiago del Estero, bending up towards the corner of three countries at the Cataratas de Iguazú, back down the curves of the Río Paraná until her conjunction with her sister the Río Uruguay, flowing, wider and slower, through the estuary of the Delta del Tigre, into the Río de la Plata, and out to the Atlantic.

The Plata River basin drains about 1/4 of the South American continent, my teacher said by way of a conclusion.

As my father continues to speak the map-memory of the republic fuses onto my view of the thousands of people in the country's capital. My mother reaches towards me at this point, caresses my knees and grabs my small hand tightly in her large warmer one. I look down. Her face is wet with tears and sweat and I know that she is listening too. I imagine that she must be experiencing a process of picturing Argentina through my father's words just like me. The feeling is too much, yet I cannot get enough of it. I wish my father would stop and yet his words are my lifeline, they convey sense and reason upon everything around me, creating order from chaos. Dizzy in the middle of such a transformation, I hold my mother's hand and look left and right in a wide circle. Being held by my mother, although it is just by the hand, protects me, allows me to keep listening to my father's important words.

Suddenly, I notice that even more men are climbing onto the trees. It seems as if they should brake, or bend at least, under all that weight, but they do not—they hold their unusual bloom of male bodies and limbs with solid gray trunks and branches. Still retaining the shifting image of Argentina and all of its people juxtaposed onto the Plaza, the heads bobbing below me begin to look again like an undulating sea of humanity. But it is not quite like a sea of people. It is more like a sky of people below me, as if the sky and the sea have switched places and I, above that expanse, on my father's shoulders, am submerged in the waters of the ocean, looking down through the surface into the sky as it touches the earth. At the far end of the Plaza de Mayo, the Casa Rosada hovers between two worlds, overseeing its followers, encompassing all time, as people from the past join those present in an afternoon that has overcome gravity.

Feeling my father's strong hands on my thin legs, I momentarily let go of my mother's hand and grab hold of my father's hair, which is curly like mine, tightly in my little hands. I realize that there is no need to worry; my parents are solidly there with me and I am in their grips. Then I too begin to shout for Perón.

Juan and Isabel finally emerged, miniscule on the Presidential Balcony of the Casa Rosada. The Plaza de Mayo exploded. I could not hear a word Perón said, so I kept singing ¡Viva Perón! ¡Viva Perón! until my ears and my throat were hoarse and numb and I could no longer tell if any sound was coming out of my mouth. But by then I did not care about that or anything else—for I was there, and I could see Perón!

When my maternal great-grandmother Gitl Frydman took the boat in 1939 and sailed away from the Baltic Coast, I ceased being a Polish Jew. She was the last of my relatives to leave. You are Jewish, we are a Jewish family, my father always said. I never knew what he meant. And yet. You know now, you say, and of course are right. We are Polish Jews who left Lublin and Warsaw between the European War and Hitler's War, and did not survive. I have become a ghost, drawing traces from past lives. My language changes as often as my port of arrival; useless ones are discarded without thought.

I have often wondered about that ship, the last boat to leave Poland before all routes were closed. An ellipsis between two worlds, the rising and setting suns, the unidirectional arrow of the compass, a wake of steam and ripples in the sea. Old... New: are there words to bridge such distance? Three months of ocean from cherished despair to blind hope. Polish, Yiddish, German, French, Flemish and who knows how many other tongues afloat before confounding with America's. Who was aboard that ship, who were those people? What instruments did they use to measure the space created by their leaving? Was the Polish national soccer team on that ship? Was a courteous gentleman with a very unusual sense of humor named M. Witold on that ship?

When my maternal great-grandmother arrived in Argentina, she moved in with her son, my Zeide Pedro, who had been trying to get her to follow him to South America ever since he had left ten years earlier. Everyone called her *La bizca rusa* and if you saw any of the pictures that have survived of her you would see why, my mother tells me (in Spanish) when I come home from college one year for my mother's birthday. Even though she wasn't Russian, she had nothing to do with Russia, they still called her *rusa*, they called us all *rusos*, it didn't matter where you were from, if you were Jewish you were a *ruso*. She lived with your grandfather, and then with your grandfather and your grandmother, once they married, and then with your grandparents and their first two children, Carlos and I, my mother says, until her death in 1949. *La bizca rusa* was the most religious member of our family, hard and cold, and always a little out of place with that strange cross-eyed look of hers and her off-balanced walk, as if she had never really made it off the ship. She scared me when I was a little girl, my mother says, with that loud voice like a man's and those hands curved and knobbed as talons, talons that would reach out and grip you whenever you went near her. She'd grab you and hug you to show her love, but frightening, really, they way she used to squeeze my thin arms and shake me as if she wanted to dislodge something. She never wanted to leave Lublin, that's what I understood, my mother explains, the baths and the other religious stuff, especially the women and their morning and late afternoon talks, like birds chirping in a tree, but finally she realized that she didn't have a choice, so she left. Nobody who didn't leave survived.

She always wore a wig, my mother adds, as if that said it all. She always wore that awful wig that must have been so hot, like nylon on your head, even as she got older, when she was so old that she couldn't walk anymore. She'd sit in the kitchen all day long listening to the radio, *la bizca rusa*, waiting for one of her grandchildren to enter so she could snatch them in her talons and yell something in their ear about her new country in Yiddish, shaking you and yelling as if you were going deaf instead of her. I see her as my mother talks, sitting on her little wooden stool in the kitchen, leaning back against the wall, the *mate* and the scorching pot of water on the table in front of her, perched like a raptor in some forgotten zoo. Waiting on that wooden stool, more and more out of place each day, staring off into that cross-eyed space of hers, perpetually off-balance and seasick, still looking through the haze of her transatlantic leaving.

SeaMark: An elevated object
serving as a beacon to mariners.

The Cape Cod Bike Trail follows the old Cape Cod Railway parallel to a line of telephone poles. The land is narrow out there, the Atlantic on one side, Cape Cod Bay on the other. The wind blows from west to east, leans heavily on the stubborn conifers, combing them towards the sea. My health held up for most of the weekend; I only had to make one or two emergency sprints to the outhouse near the path per day. People on mountain bikes passed occasionally, smiled, said hello. You commented that the only time New Englanders seemed to let their guard down is on holiday weekends and even then, never too much.

It was the end of summer of our year in Providence together. We spent two nights in a bed and breakfast near Eastham called The SeaMark. Our room downstairs had wood ceilings, a fire stove and a stack of nature magazines and bird books on one of the night tables by the bed. I chose the side with the books and the magazines. They reminded me of the *National Geographics* that we started receiving when we moved to San Diego in 1978 and which are still in boxes in my parents' garage there. You read a British mystery on the other side of the bed while I studied maps of bird migration, tracing the great journeys of the world's major migratory birds.

On our hike the next day I saw a pair of Orange-crowned Warblers from the trail, calling from the lower branches of a juniper, and recognized them from an article in the *Audubon Monthly* I had read at the bed and breakfast. They were migratory birds, off-course by some 2,000 miles. Their high-pitched staccato trill first caught my attention: I knew it as a warbler's, but it was a song I had never heard before. We stopped, looked into the trees. Then I spotted them, small olive-colored birds with yellow undertail coverts and the unmistakable tawny-orange crown (only on the male, that is; the coloring on the female, like that of most species, was drabber overall, and the crown was absent). Those two warblers should have been in the salt-water marshes off the Gulf of Mexico, along the coast of Texas or Louisiana, down in the Florida keys, or in the estuaries of Mexico or Central America, instead of on the tip of Massachusetts. They were vagrants—fallouts: tricked by wind currents blind to the principle of desired destination. Instead of arriving in their southern wintering grounds, the Orange-crowned Warblers had strayed completely off their flyway and found themselves pecking for insects on the branches of spruce trees and other conifers which they should have left far behind in their northern breeding grounds.

At lunch we both knew what the other was thinking. Last year at this time your father had had his triple by-pass surgery. It fit somehow, that it had fallen on Labor Day. Your father, who had taught math in high school for thirty-seven years without calling in sick one single day. Had accumulated three years of unused sick leave. Early September: soon the leaves would be turning out on the Cape. And us still living so far from our families. Fish and chips was scrod and greasy. I loved it; you shook your head. Through the windows of the restaurant we could see the grass growing on the dunes and the wooden fences: they matched your mental picture of a New England coastline perfectly, you said. Outside, it felt entirely like Autumn—the wind biting—and our upcoming Christmas trip to California seemed a long time away.

I love that Wallace but he was a sad man, you said, continuing a conversation about poets and places.

Over breakfast at the inn, the morning we were about to return to Providence, I let you answer "California" for both of us when the proprietors asked where we were from. The woman smiled. Said she had never been there; she only knew her coast, but of course had seen California on the television and in the movies many times. Must be nice, she said. We all smiled.

When I think of our time out there, I realize that I liked living on the East Coast, wearing dress shoes and slacks, keeping to ourselves all year long.

It was always late in the day when my father returned from work. A number of years ago I spent a summer with him in France, analyzing everything. The last time we were there had been for his post-doc in 1972, the four of us in Orsay, before the return to Argentina, before the new series of unexpected leavings. Now it was Paris and it was just him and I, my father working in a lab for two months and I studying French—relearning it, really—after my freshman year of college. The shadows that stretched further than anyone could see, the only constant. There is grandeur in my father's science, blueprints written in the language of mathematics. Equations to unravel quantitative questions. *La física del viejo.*

* * *

The uncertainty principle states that position and momentum in a given direction cannot both be simultaneously determined to an exact degree.

* * *

The signs of decay were evident: a certain slant of light, the emptiness amid the medieval constructions. In the mornings, I visited monuments. At lunch, we met to eat quietly among French workers in dark restaurants where fixed menus were served. I was shy and did not do well on my own back then; he, meanwhile, seemed lost in abstractions. After lamb and red wine, bread and cheese, he would sum up our situation with single phrases and strange translations. Those small dark restaurants near the Gare de Lyons where we had our midday meals, he said, were replete with the melancholy of departure.

As if this city had no name, no history, no context, and all he saw was himself projected unto it.

* * *

When an electron jumps from one energy level to another in an atom, it is said to make a quantum leap before it settles into a new, stable radius. But it is not a radius, really, for the planetary model is not quite accurate for the atomic world.

* * *

Two men, diminished, rotating around each other. Outside, banners and train smoke in the background, suggesting wind, direction, a different nature. I pointed to the shadows, all the way across the city, the canvas, the era. Ghosts, he answered, satisfied, already looking towards the next derivation. How could I pay him back? I was eighteen. Simple, he said, take me to a nineteen and a half *toques* restaurant in Eugene-sûr-Bains. He picked the place that quickly, the answer voiced with the speed of technology, like the solution to a basic problem he had memorized from a table of integrals in his youth. I looked it up in the Biblioteque Nationale the next day and discovered that Eugene-sûr-Bains is a town in the Petites Pyrénées, near the Spanish border. The place, and the famous restaurant to which it is apparently home, remains for me a name on a map.

* * *

Electrons must be thought of not spatially "sharp" (only on average being at a certain distance away from the center of the atom), but rather as wave packets that exist in quantum states of given physical observables such as energy and angular momentum.

* * *

A moment that swallows everything around it is said to exist in all languages. Such a moment is known as a translator's utopia, the dream of the bricklayers of Babel.

* * *

Still, empirical data informs us that an electron will never be found in the intermediary state between two energy levels. Planck, Einstein and Dirac, among others (e.g., Heisenberg, Schrodinger) created an entire branch of physics, quantum mechanics, to describe this leap. Invisible and ineffable, like the matter of thought.

I am looking for the visionary south today, the man bent over his blue guitar. I know why he's your favorite now, straddling long verses and modernity, learning where to aim the lens, having to pick the century, the continent, then accepting our own here and now. A matter of what you are willing to give up, you say, to see things as they are. A Spanish serenade becomes a lie, it is no song, no melody with which to fly. Walking on taut strings, metal pulled and plucked, leaves us undone. Not to dissect, but to reshape, it must be opened, again and again. Ruins—our only past.

Women become cities and men in waves become the sea.

Can your words lead me to a painting, a poem, a figure connected with dots across the bluest map? The ship is a parenthesis and so is this, colors decided on your tongue, the space between you and me, yesterday and today. There is never such a thing as tomorrow.

I did as you told me to do, searched his rhymes, the blue guitar and I are one, he said. Meanwhile the album spun, the music too a language for me to learn, you say to me, come in and stay. The other album is before you, turn the page, see yourself in me, is the only way I know to read his line. The other, the same, male and female become one. He saw Atlantis from his florid keys, you Rome from the Central Coast, me Silver Rivers before Providence. But the columns have long since stood alone, abandoned temples that abandoned their own walls.

Did he believe, as you and I? Did he find his visionary south? His north wind blew from above only on maps, in life it hit him on the back, swirling snow whitening fading blue, to turn his face was the normal thing to do. We too felt New

England winds, a naked elm outside our window, turned west to see what neither one of us could hide. Nevertheless, I love the rhapsody of things as they are and thank him for his pine and for his jay, imagined as they are.

The teacher avoided our eyes when she told us that we could go home early; somehow, everyone knew it was not something to celebrate. Although no one was capable of saying what had actually occurred, everyone seemed to know, as if the news was simply there, in the air, traveling at frequencies that our ears could not hear but which our bodies could interpret easily enough. Even the kids towards the back of the class were silent, their usual jokes and capers suppressed in the communal shock. *Se pueden retirar, niños, ya, se cierra la escuela, por lo menos por el día de hoy, vuélvanse directamente a casa, vayan.* And the school emptied out and closed behind us and everyone left quietly, heading their own separate ways.

There was almost no traffic, even on the busy avenues such as Juramento and Cabildo, and I saw only one person the whole way home: a middle-aged woman with groceries in a netted bag, her dark hair pulled tightly up in a bun, wearing a plain black dress and flat-heeled shoes, hurrying efficiently along, staring down at the sidewalk. The stores were locked up as if everyone had shut down and deserted the city. Belgrano was a very lively neighborhood; with cafés at every corner and restaurants and storefronts on every block, it was normally crowded at all hours of the day, especially near Barrancas, not far from where we lived on Calle 3 de Febrero. I had never seen anything like this. The corrugated iron shutters were drawn and thick chains secured every door and window. It was cold and the overcast sky above the roofs of the tall buildings loomed ominously, as if it were about to descend on the empty streets below it. Even the usual bright colors of the geraniums hanging off the balconies on the side streets seemed dulled and muted by the grayness of the day. I decided to try the park where I went every day after school to play soccer; it too was completely empty, no sign of the other kids, the dogs running after them, or the old men and women who always sat on the benches around the plaza. I stood alone on the grass for a while in the middle of the park; it seemed so strange, unreal, without its regular visitors. How places change when the people we associate with them are not there, especially when their disappearance is sudden and unexpected. I shivered in my school uniform, under the ashen sky, and looked around as if to make sure to register the emptiness, somehow knowing that I should never forget that day. As if I already knew then, afraid and by myself, that things would never be quite the same. I ran the rest of the way home—Perón was dead.

I insist that the distance between the two continents is negligible. This appears to touch a nerve. You lash out from the other side of the kitchen table, argue that I am trying to do what a telephone line or a television transmission can accomplish instantaneously these days. The futile repetition involved in challenging time. So you place the blue guitarist in the Florida Keys, a different summer, opposite hemispheres, genres. I know two of your heroes reside there, as Elizabeth Bishop's map poems and Wallace Stevens' levels of language turn you insistent, create foundations where I see only reflections. Whereas I place him (the blue guitarist) in Buenos Aires, not far from the port of the Río de la Plata. *Entre San Telmo y la Costanera Norte—*

* * *

The loud, blackened vessels that pitch anchor in the port of Santa María de los Buenos Aires bring to its piers the industrial harvest of both hemispheres, the colors and sounds of the four races, the salt and iodine of the seven seas. From there, following the course of the Riachuelo as far as the refrigerated warehouses, you can see the young bulls and calves waiting, crowded, in the sun. Orchestral trains enter and leave the city at all hours of the day.

* * *

I hear a tune played on an accordion, elegant male gestures leading female heels stomping rhythm and determination on a dance floor in La Boca. Dramatic masks offered at the junction, then, there. The Keys droop down, the Equator melts them (in this at least—its tendency towards primitivism through heat—we agree). And they too disembark at the sound of a silvery destination. After all, you add, who can resist the temptation of places named after precious metals: *El alto destino de la tierra Que-de-puro-metal-saca-su-nombre.* Whether it be the Tiber or the Seine, it does not matter, they all lead to the Río de la Plata: currents carry immigrants drawn by promises of fields of ore where the category of foreigner becomes unstable. The waters come in, lap waves of time, introducing diverse (a fancy word for random? we wonder) elements to a new form. A tango scratched from the throats of turn-of-the-century Europeans in a horizon-less continent. And now one must make do in northern lands, cold and productive, with a suitcase of books and albums, thankful that the blue guitarist still hovers there: as needle touches vinyl, the translator cites and copies: so distance shrinks and time disappears.

The summer before I changed my major in college, I worked at S-Cubed, my father's company in San Diego. My job was to test a computer program emulating the effects of space plasma on the materials used on the hull of satellites and to help write the manual for the program. I found and figured out how to play several computer games on the company's mainframe. I improved my skills at the UNIX operating system so I could switch back and forth between the games and the simulation I was supposed to be working on with the click of a key. When I was growing up, physics was not just a science, nor merely another profession—it was a philosophy, a way to construct models that explained the world and the universe. But these models did more than explain the world: they held it up. It was impossible to conceive of a world without physics, as if the world would simply cease to exist if it did not have models to define it. As if the world and the models that physics created to represent it were one and the same. The mathematical formulas, the Xs and Ys, the sines and cosines, the integrals and derivatives, the logarithms and differential equations provided every aspect of the vocabulary needed to articulate a model so powerful that it could tell us who we were at every level, from molecular interactions to the very mysteries of the cosmos, its origin and design.

After I left for college my father set up an extra bookcase in my old room, so that every night of the summer that I worked at S-Cubed, living with my parents again for those three months, I'd look up from my bed as I tried to fall asleep and see his books on the new shelves, illuminated even in the dark by an outside light right by my window. I'd stare at my father's books and think about the intricacies of my father's physics, a field whose depths I could only begin to imagine.

I'd lie there and gaze at the spines of my father's books, reading the titles sideways to myself as if they were in a foreign tongue, as indecipherable as the secret manuals of a forgotten alchemist: Wannier's *Solid State Theory*, *Física atómica* de Max Born, *Quantum Mechanics* by Philip Stehle, Gosiorowicz's *Elemental Particle Physics*, *Mathematical Physics* by Donald H. Menzel.

I played indoor soccer at lunch twice a week with my father while I worked at his company. They even had a locker room where you could shower and change after exercising. I finished the program testing and the manual for the space plasma simulation, made very good money after only two years of college, but I still changed my major to literature when I went back to Berkeley that Fall. The models were not as easy to disassemble.

NAMES & TONGUES

I don't even know which language to use. *¿Qué carajo estoy haciendo hablando en inglés?* It's how you use the language, you say, and of course are right. Carlos Gardel was the godfather of the genre, the man who put Argentina on the map, and Astor Piazzolla, with his sharp experimental compositions, updated the form with his renovations in the 1960s and 70s, but the one who speaks to me, as he spoke to my parents, is the golden-voiced singer who came in between, who looked back to the canons of the 1920s and 30s not with nostalgia but with promise: *el nene con la voz de oro,* Julio Sosa. *Al viejo estilo.* If I could interpret the quality of his voice, import *El último café.* His arms raised like those of Perón in exile, his tonal complexities speaking of the caudillo's return. Singing: *Al mundo le falta un tornillo, / ¡va a haber que llamar a un mecánico, / para ver si lo puede arreglar!*

   To go back, to meet the descendants of the labyrinth, of the tango. To see the face of my Argentine ghost, as my father would say. Another singer whose funeral entourage defined a country, reminiscent of the day nearly thirty years before on which flowers rained down on Gardel's last journey through the city of Buenos Aires. The Southern Hemisphere's reflection of my life in the United States, where I'm sustained by long-distance phone calls and warehouse supermarkets, libraries and computers, books on walls to cushion hard surfaces and sharp angles. Our daughter will have blue eyes, maybe green. She will not drink *mate.* But her hair will curl like yours, just wait and see, you say. Still, the ghost is here, not there. There I speak regularly with Martín Fierro, eat dinner at midnight. Go to the corner café in Belgrano where you and I drink short espressos with a splash of milk, discuss inflation and Kafka surrounded by faded black and white photographs of soccer heroes from the 1950s and 60s: Labruna (#10), Lusteau (#11) and the goalkeeper Carrizo.

Everything closed for thirty days. Bars, cafés, grocery stores, restaurants, bakeries, pharmacies, pizzerias, schools, pharmacies, hospitals, theatres, everything. Only later did we realize that half the country celebrated behind closed doors while the other half mourned. *Los muchachos peronistas...* I saw my father very little the next year. He stood in line for three days, mostly in the rain, to say good-bye to the General's corpse. My sister and I looked for him on television, but saw only women in black fighting off armed guards to throw themselves on an open coffin framed in red and yellow flowers. The camera scanned the line of mourners for dozens of city blocks. People stood or leaned against each other, packed closely against the sides of the buildings to protect themselves from the rain, and no one appeared to move at all. It was a very strange kind of line as my sister and I saw it, the gray faces of the men and women, young and old alike, with beige raincoats and black hats or scarves and the gray water constantly falling, as if the grime and dirt of the entire city was dripping on those poor stationary people. And I remember, too, that however hard I tried I could not make out their expressions: they seemed to be neither there by choice nor by force, but rather as if they had always been meant to be in that line, waiting for city block after city block, out in the elements like that.

I was too young to go with my father. I wondered where he peed for those three days. In the period immediately following Perón's death, the flowers piled up in the capital higher and higher. They grew into hills and kept growing until it became the first occurrence in modern geological time in which the fertile pampas witnessed mountains anywhere in the vicinity of the Province of Buenos Aires. They pushed against the edge of the Río de la Plata, dragging the country's namesake across the fields and then through the streets of the city, into the port and the wide salty river and out into the Atlantic. A few years ago I asked my father about Perón in the Presidential casket. He looked bad, my father said.

Even the few scattered Spanish words, desperate to conjure Argentine images, port-side smells along the *Costanera* and afternoon visits to my great-aunt in her cold patio, are only illusions. Which one is the ghost? I thought you were a Polish Jew, you say, alluding to a tailor in Lublin and a watchmaker from Warsaw. I never learned the Yiddish my grandparents used when they wanted to hide something from the kids. Yiddish became strange noises that meant a friend or a relative had had sex. The secret tongue of the elders, as you like to say. I found my grandfather reading a Yiddish paper in Buenos Aires one day. (*Di Yidische Zaitung.*) I was extremely impressed. I didn't know you spoke Chinese, Zeide, I said to him. I never learned Yiddish, we left. *Zihch ronos* is what we have now. I did not speak a word of English in the fifth grade, but by the time I was playing four-square on the junior high playground in San Diego, no one could tell a part of me still lived in another country. A *ruach* running around, pretending to be like all the other children on the school's blacktop.

* * *

The successive Jewish migrations to Argentina (1889, 1905, 1920, 1938), first out to the colonies and later into the cities, led to the creation of numerous printed papers, including *Viderkol* (El Eco), *Der Idisher Fonograph* (El Fonógrafo Judío), and *Di Folks Shtime* (La Voz del Pueblo), all founded in 1898; the first Jewish newspaper in Spanish was *El Sionista* (The Zionist, 1904). These were followed by *Der Avangard* (La Vanguardia, 1908); the Zionist-Socialist *Broit un Ehre* (Pan y Dignidad, 1909); *Idisher Colonist in Arguentine* (El Colono Israelita en Argentina, 1909), directed by agriculturists; *Di Yidische Zaitung* (El Diario Israelita, 1914), which inaugurates Argentina's Jewish professional journalism[1]; and *Di Presse* (1918), which published Freud and Marx in Yiddish in Argentina, before either were available in Spanish. There were also many cultural magazines, including *Vida Nuestra* (Our Life, 1917-1923), *Judaica* (1933-1946), *Davar* (begun in 1945 by the Sociedad Hebraica Argentina), *Davke, Majshavot, Heredad, La Luz* (1931), *Raíces* (which had two periods), *Comentario* (the magazine of the Instituto Judío Argentino de Cultura e Información), *Renovación, Tiempo*, and *Plural*, among others. *Oif di Bregn fun Plata* (A orillas del Plata), the first Yiddish anthology of Jewish Argentine writers, was published in 1919, the same year in which I. L. Péretz's stories were published in Spanish translation in Argentina.

---

[1] In 1942, it is a writer from *Di Yidische Zaitung* who provides detective Lönnrot with a crucial insight to solve a quadruple murder case framed within a Cabbalistic labyrinth in the outskirts of Buenos Aires.

I was once a center-half, played my days out on a Southern California field, imagined by a Jewish physicist between the algorithms of a *Juventud Peronista* meeting. Seeking to defy chronologies, he projects far into his children's lives. Coaches his son's soccer team in the north, raises a daughter—my sister—combative like himself to practice American law. So much to think about in the back of a Ford Torino. Sees his son running drills around orange cones, teaches him never to let the ball get too far when he dribbles, sets up a row of balls for the boy to practice shooting at goal, designs the small uniforms for the entire team, reserves #5 for his son.

Standing by our miniature version, far away still. The hide, its content, the game and the wine and always a song to blame fortune. In an eight by ten plot of lawn behind our rented condominium in Boulder, surrounded by clearly demarcated parking spots and other small plots of neatly trimmed grass just like ours. Inside, a suitcase filled with dictionaries, the widest river in the world, aunts sipping *mate* in Yiddish, a chocolate hazelnut cake in the shade of a rubber tree plant. Out here, the ceaseless rumbling from nearby avenues, accelerating motors and screeching breaks against the snow-peaked mountains to the west. Can you hear the balladeer as he once sang: *Venía la carne con cuero, / la sabrosa carbonada, / mazamorra bien pisada, / los pasteles y el güen vino; / pero ha querido el destino / que todo aquello acabara.*

I close my eyes and see geraniums flowing on balconies above, a mechanical tram and an old woman dressed in black struggling with meshed shopping bags. The south is not blue and white, the haze is only natural, time and smog: the widest avenue in the world could do no less. It is impossible without you, take my hand in yours, fingers never meant to play waltzes on grand pianos in an empty house. Empty but not abandoned, one of us is quick to add. The neighborhood dogs bark again, acknowledge what the rusted bars in front with the wild rose bushes and the dilapidated whitewashed walls cannot. Who would have thought that our daughter would choose violin? Imagining what might have been if the coup had not occurred is more tempting—more dangerous—than anything else. A place where the threshold between reason and what lies beyond is torn down, undone in a shift that allows me to go back and live the life we left. Almost as if we had not left, as if my Argentine self continued living there of its own accord, as if I could change a lifetime with a few words. Loose notes, gathered here for the moment. Dreaming of living (there) instead of leaving. Living (here) because we left. Roaming through rooms of the past, left, wrong and forgotten. Almost.

And when the old man draws the lyrics to a close, strums the guitar no more; when the balladeer fades as rising smoke always does, we hear the first notes of a new song, let words and bodies touch at last.

One day the security guards and the thugs took over, it was that simple—that is how my father describes it. The scientists and the intellectuals were out. For months the three branches of the military—*La Marina, El Ejército, La Fuerza Aérea*—waited patiently in their ranks, painstakingly cleaning, inspecting and buffing every item of their arsenal, from the semiautomatic weapons to the fighter planes which would require only a few low flights over the Casa Rosada to make their intentions clear. The officers had time to train the draftees, while the colonels and the generals had time to get their manicures, preparing their hands for the delicate gestures and commands necessary to deal with moral enemies. Rifles sparkling in the sun, ready to pierce the fecund pampas, the jagged coastline and the cave-dotted Andean peaks. Finally, the people were ready for them, their march could begin.

I missed the occasional chauffeured ride next to my father in the Ford Torino. I loved how the chauffeur could stick his arm out the window and put a siren on the roof of the car to avoid getting stuck at red lights. How the air conditioner was turned up all the way, the windows rolled down, just to impress a physicist's nine-year-old son. But after the coup even our fourth grade political analogies—comparing key figures to positions on the soccer field, arguing about the scoring capacity of left and right wingers, the importance of strong mid-fielders—came to an abrupt end.

* * *

On March 24, 1976, the Junta of the Chiefs, led by Army General Jorge Rafael Videla, Navy Admiral Emilio Eduardo Massera and Air Force Brigadier Orlando Ramón Agosti, assumed control of the country and began the Process of National Reorganization: *El Proceso*. Videla was named president of the nation on March 26.

* * *

We quickly ceased playing at being adults by echoing discussions and comments heard at home, without anyone having to tell us to do so. Regardless, the school courtyard remained oddly the same: at 8:00 a.m. we stood in straight lines for the flag raising and singing of the national anthem, and for fifteen quick minutes during the morning and afternoon recesses the girls played hopscotch and the boys chased each other around the ancient rubber plant tree. We took our cue from our parents, went back to our long-hand division. Torture meant that they could throw you in a pen with rabid dogs who knew to go for your testicles first. For the longest time that seemed more frightening than the concept of disappearing someone.

Translation is a contamination, a constant giving and taking and ending up where one thought one had already been, only to discover it as new again. The disease metaphor is useful here, as it helps us recall that neither body is pure, that language is a virus, that you and I are carriers and that love resides in the few words that we manage to interchange.

With time, the simulacrum will land on solid ground. Regardless of how long it takes cartographers to map its boundaries, it too will find a continent, a place on globes, in encyclopedias. Unable to visit the original—held back by language barriers, expelled by coups—many will visit the new instead, know of the old only to the extent that it resonates in the new. With the two we may begin to make a vessel, but only if performed with a measure of efficacy.

A harp here, a delta there. Something about uncharted waters, something about separation through reproduction. Mirrors and paternity. Not a matter of discovering or conquering, not a bridge or a resolution, but a parenthesis, the only time that one (I? you? her?) can float freely in both directions, in between. Whereas the new is not really new, just as the original is not at all original. For example: Junior's enigmatic voyage through a futuristic Buenos Aires. A analogous to B, becomes B. Take a sentence, A. Already written (by another, in another's book), it will become B (it will be a translation, in another book, not quite mine, not quite yours, perhaps hers). But to go from A to B, its elements must be set free—A must be deformed, exploded, allowed to become loose pieces, no longer A, not yet B. In the moment of transition, from A to B, A and B both cease to exist as such. And yet, at the same time, there is still A, even on its way to being B. And so it goes, down and down the line. Besides, it is the only way to be.

It also means, here and later, when this is all over, the experience of walking along the streets of a city that is mine and in which, nevertheless, I will always be a foreigner. And the fact that I have yet to find a place in the world in which I do not have this feeling. Signifying the conflict itself, searching there for the white knots of experience.

How they arc their necks to look backwards, tails close to their haunches, as paranoid as us. They too spin in place, change shapes, reach and slide towards each other. Pulling like gravity. Maybe just the mane is blue. Soon they will imitate violence, bite the other's shoulder, confuse flesh with memory. Undo the name we give them. Dreaming us as we dream them. In the morning the blue horses are at rest, or running in the snow: days seen all at once, angles in a landscape that speaks ages. Avoiding heavy red, instinctual rays. The sun blinding like bleach.

Teeth marks remain, no amount of clothing or talking can hide them. What we wouldn't give for bay windows. If one could unthread distance, assume a second floor. Reckoning in the snow that reminds us of milk but tastes nothing like it, everything in between. The accordion in the coffee cup, a lighted candle, the weight of paper. Bottle of wine, clapping to the music, searching for level ground: something to remind us tones ascend from shapes.

And in the evening, the colors our skins create, then. Always. The echo of blue horses. Their shadow on our walls.

Preguntales a ellos, a ver qué dicen,
my mother always says...

She takes his arm in hers as they walk along, leaning on each other as they read the names and dates on each stone before going on to the next. The rain has let up, at least for now, but it is still cold, windy and overcast. Neither says a word.

I know that day of theirs so well: the train ride from Penn Station to Philadelphia; asking the bored attendant in the booth for directions (I can hear my grandmother using the few English words she has learned with such assertiveness that the attendant cannot help but understand and point them in the right direction); the slow uneventful walk through the suburb with the non-descript houses, large green lawns and prominent garages on either side. The arched brick entrance to the cemetery and the cats playing nearby. Then, after entering, the inadvertent kicking of the moist leaves that do not rustle or make any sound at all. A sense of moving further and further into a world of silence; as if every step brought them closer and closer to the place where the souls of the corpses decomposing below have gone. All alone they read the gravestones and try to decipher the isolated words summarizing the lives of all those people, many of whom—like the one whose stone they are looking for—ended their lives so far from where they began. I know it so well, their roaming through the plots set aside for the dead, looking for the final resting place of my great grandfather Abraham.

My Zeide Pedro's goatee is not as white as I will come to know it, but already it is a rich silver. His hair impeccably combed back, it gleams like wax, and he wears a heavy gray and black parka over his short but solid body (an Old World body to go with an Old World man, as my sister says). My Bube Cata, her face set like stone, leads them with that look of hers that lets you know that there is more behind her pale blue eyes than she will ever let on. Thinking the entire time about Abraham, Pedro's father, and of how he ended up there, of all places. Looking for something that might help to explain the decisions he made in his life; something to help unravel the mystery—or part of it, at least—of what became of him and his life with his brother Hirsch in Philadelphia, while their own lives took such a different course in Buenos Aires. Wondering if Abraham selected the burial ground himself before his death, or if it was selected for him. Wondering about the recent turns in their own lives, living and working in New York now.

They had arrived in Philadelphia the day before and had gone immediately to investigate Abraham and Hirsch's old neighborhood. They looked for anyone who could help them fill in some of the missing pieces of the family story. Knocking on random doors, my grandmother's arm always in my grandfather's, the two leaning slightly on each other, they narrowed their search to a busy city block near downtown, and then to a plain eight-story brick building. They spoke with several neighbors who still remembered the handsome Polish Jew who had come from Lublin to live with his brother Hirsch on the fifth floor, the one who had nearly drowned in the freezing Atlantic when the boat went down near Ellis Island, one old woman who was especially friendly and invited them into her apartment said over tea. And how he caught pneumonia and how it took six months before he made it back to this world. Their host must have been in her eighties, short with thin wisps of transparent blue hair; they listened to her as long as she was willing to talk. She seemed happy to be speaking Yiddish with the younger couple, who could have been her own children, in age, at least, as she said. She confirmed what my grandparents already knew about Hirsch: that he owned a small shoe factory, that Abraham worked there with him from the moment he recovered from the pneumonia until the end of his life. Pedro looks just like Abraham, she said, looking at Cata knowingly. Then she told my grandparents about the young woman who nursed Abraham during his pneumonia, the one who lived downstairs from the brothers, right here in the same building, you know, she added with a certain tone and smile that told them that there was probably more to it, that Hirsch, Abraham and the nurse were probably once the topic of a number of conversations just like this one over tea in that same living room. Eh, but that's a lifetime ago, the old woman said, as if talking about the dead had suddenly tired her, and quickly told them what they needed to know so they might continue their search: that Abraham had died from cancer—colon, or prostate, she couldn't remember—some five years after his older brother Hirsch, and that he was buried in Montefiore. She hurried them out, no longer quite as friendly as she had been just a few minutes before.

And so they have found the entrance to the cemetery, after walking through the suburb in the rain. They have gone under the arched entrance, on the graveled path up the hill, leaning on each other, arm in arm. They have traveled the distance from stone to stone, from name to name, away from the path, through layers of leaves that have made all movement slow and deliberate. Then, finally in front of the right gravestone, the Star of David sinking into the earth, they have read the name and the dates they expected to find.

My Zeide Pedro and my Bube Cata have only been in the States for a few weeks. It is the fall of 1966. They have just installed themselves in a small apartment that doubles as their sewing and repairs shop in the Bronx. It is the beginning of a time that, standing there in front of my great grandfather's gravestone, will bring surprises they cannot possibly predict. They do not know that in the next ten years (by the time my parents, my sister and I will join them in

New York, leaving Argentina right after the coup) they will eventually have affluent customers in Manhattan who will pay high prices for detailed alterations and custom-made patterns; that in time they will make enough money to visit Poland (where they will find that the neighborhood that my Zeide remembered from his childhood in Lublin now consists of tall drab tenement buildings without a trace of the Jewish shops and street vendors that once thrived there); that they will be able to travel to France, England, Spain, Italy, Egypt and Israel in chartered trips with older tourists (even before they were old enough to be in such groups they always preferred these and had tremendous fun with the seniors), where they will begin their collection of small dolls and trinkets to remind them of all the places in the world they have visited— an international still-life of traveled memories arranged on the shelves of their living room cabinet.

On that day in Montefiore, however, Pedro and Cata have no idea that any of these things still await them. They have found Abraham's gravestone, but not Hirsch's, or that of anyone else whose name they might recognize (and of course not Abraham's wife, Gitl, my great grandmother who was too religious to leave Lublin for America, so she let her husband go alone to work and send money back). Just Abraham, surrounded by strangers; no explanations, only the place marking where his life ended. Abraham Kalmen Leip Frydman, they read again, as if wanting to be sure. My grandmother pulls away from my grandfather and one after the other they bring two fingers to their lips and lean over to touch Abraham's name on the cold stone with those same two fingers. Then their arms rejoin and they turn around and head back through the cold mist towards their new home in New York.

Wait a second, you say, I need to get all these names straight. At least those of your grandparents. Okay, I'll start with my mother's side, those I know, but I can't promise that it'll make much sense. Let us make us a name. My maternal grandfather is Schmil Peseigh Frydman; that's in Yiddish. In Polish, it's more or less the same but with different spelling (according to my Bube Cata). When he arrived in Argentina, it became Samuel Pascual Frydman, but he disliked the sound of both his first and middle names, so he called himself Pedro Frydman. In English, Schmil Peseigh is Samuel Passover, but while he lived in New York, he dropped the middle name, and went by Samuel Frydman in all his documents. I call him Zeide Pedro, although in Spanish it's abuelo, as you know. It's one of the few Yiddish idioms that I've retained.

My Zeide Pedro left Poland for Argentina in 1929. He traveled from Lublin to Warsaw and on to Gdynia by train. There, he boarded a smallish steamship that made its way from the Gulf of Gdansk to the Baltic Sea, northwest through Swedish and Danish straights, southwest through the North Sea and west across the English Channel to Cherbourg, France, where he transferred onto the third class S.S. Almanzora steamship of the English Royal Mail Line: *La mala real inglesa*. This vessel crossed the Atlantic, with brief stops in La Coruña, Vigo, Oporto and Lisboa on the Iberian Peninsula, in Pernambuco, Bahía, Rio de Janerio and Santos in Brazil and Montevideo in Uruguay, reaching the end of the line in the port of Buenos Aires, where Pedro disembarked. He slowly learned Spanish, then, in Argentina—in the *conventillo* where he first lived in Villa Crespo, in the cafés of Chacarita, in the streets of El Once, in meetings near Boedo, at his first jobs in Flores—at seventeen. Only he, of everyone in our family, still speaks broken Spanish with a strong Eastern European accent and makes frequent mistakes in gender and tense. All this we know.

My maternal grandmother, Pedro's wife, is Jane Gitl Silverstein Frydman in Yiddish, Chana Gitla Silverstein Frydman in Polish, Juana Catalina Silverstein Frydman in Spanish and Jane Frydman in English, but she has always gone by Cata, short for Catalina. I call her Bube Cata, although some distant cousins of mine in Argentina, who come from Russia, call her Bobe. This too we know. My Bube Cata eventually became a *modiste*, learned to seamstress with world-class expertise, although she apparently never received any training at all in this work. Whenever I ask her about it she tells me how Pedro learned from Abraham as an adolescent in Lublin (though this is doubtful, especially given what I have gathered about Abraham's life around that time), or else she starts to talk about her clients, the ones from the Upper East side when they lived in New York, or the ones who drive in from Miami these days and pay her in cash so she won't have to report the earnings. That is what I know and can recount.

Pedro's father, my great grandfather Abraham, was a tailor from Lublin, although he might have been a peddler, or at most a tailor's apprentice—the family stories are inconsistent here. What is known is that Abraham (Abram) left Poland well before his son, that he migrated to Philadelphia immediately following World War I, leaving his wife and five children behind. He chose Philadelphia because his brother Hirsch had moved there in 1904 and was supposedly doing very well in the shoe industry. Although Abraham's wife, my great grandmother Gitl, did not go with Abraham, apparently because of her religious beliefs, Abraham himself had no doubts about leaving the old country. He had spent most of the First World War as a prisoner in a German camp (a Polish soldier recruited and captured in 1914, during his first month of service) and wanted no more of Poland.

My maternal great grandmother, Gitl Frydman—Pedro's mother—stayed in Lublin when Abraham left, but in 1939 my Zeide convinced her, after some ten years of insistent correspondence—and helped by the fact that Abraham's letters with their few accompanying dollars had stopped arriving even sporadically from America—to join him and Cata in Argentina, where he had married my grandmother Cata the year before. Gitl became *la bizca rusa* soon after moving in with them in Chacarita. If I am not mistaken, the ship Gitl took in 1939 was the last ship allowed to carry Jews out of the northern coast of Eastern Europe. Based on a series of conversations with my grandparents in Florida, and on dates and figures gathered at the Brown and Boulder libraries, I have come to believe that Gitl shared that steam-powered crossing with the Polish national soccer team (which then spent the rest of the War in Argentina and none of whose players ever again competed in an international match, even after their return to Poland, although several did have a fruitful career in the Argentine fútbol leagues) and with a curious looking man who enjoyed shuffle board on the forward deck and introduced himself, with a slight cackle, as Count Witold (and whose little adventure abroad lasted until 1969). Thus Gitl's trans-Atlantic parenthesis.

Cata's parents, Silvia and Jaime Morgenstern (already in Spanish)—my other maternal great grandparents—made their one-way journey from Poland to Argentina in 1925. They brought with them the one daughter they had so far, Cata, who was three years old at the time. In Buenos Aires Jaime and Silvia had four additional children: Natalio, Dora, Sarah (nicknamed Coca), and Feliza, and a still-born for whom, luckily, a name had not yet been chosen. From this group the great aunts, fanatics of *mate* and *pretzelech* in inner patios. And so it went from Poland to Argentina: let us build us a city, they might have said, and did.

A few years ago, while living in Providence, I took a few days off from my work at the Brown library to see my father in Washington, D.C., where he was on a business trip. I spent most of that time at the Mall, visiting monuments named after people I learned about when we had first moved to the U.S. (I still remember how strange names like Washington and Jefferson and Lincoln sounded to my ten-year-old ears, not to mention the very idea that there were heroes in the world who I'd never heard of, and who were not San Martín and Belgrano and Sarmiento and the others whose lives I'd committed to memory during my years in elementary school in Argentina). After a day of monuments and museums, I decided to go on a brief expedition and took a train back north to Philadelphia to look for my maternal great grandfather's gravestone—just as my grandparents had some twenty-five years earlier.

I set out on an overcast morning. For the entire ride, the sites through the train window were gray, from the thick and turbulent waters of the Potomac beneath the rust-iron bridge, to the industrial sections of Baltimore and again closer to Philadelphia, to the single houses with leafless trees on the outskirts of the various towns in between the cities. It drizzled all morning; I sat in an almost empty Amtrak car, with a small bunch of daffodils that I had purchased at the train station on the seat next to me. Philadelphia and its outskirts seemed submersed in heavy clouds that had no intention of departing, but could not yet make up their mind to rid themselves of their watery contents. I got directions at my stop, and started on the fifteen-minute trek from the station to the cemetery. The October rain, combined with not seeing anyone for the duration of that short walk through a nondescript suburb, precipitated a feeling that I do not remember ever having had before or since: I felt like I could be anywhere in the world, in any city or country, at any time in my life, or of history. Under my black umbrella, looking through the falling mist for the entrance to Montefiore Cemetery, I was certain I could have walked on unnoticed and unheeded for a long time, without tiring, without feeling the need to eat or sleep, just for the sake of walking, of covering ground, of leaving it behind me and knowing that it was the continuing rhythmic motion of my legs that kept me moving.

The entrance was an unadorned rounded arch opening along a red brick wall in the middle of the block. A graveled path led slightly uphill; upon entering, one left the suburb completely behind; the many trees and stones were crowded and without any apparent order to their arrangement, unlike the perfect distribution of the houses and lawns just outside. I walked in and headed towards the center of the cemetery, reading at random the names and years on the stones amid the leafs fallen from their branches. The tombstones leant this way and that in the muddy soil, as if they were tired of being upright, as if the years, once the owners had departed from this world, weighed down on their stones instead of on them. I walked on. From under innumerable layers of damp leafs, the earth continued calling and pulling at the headstones of the lives they denoted, as if wanting to erase all evidence of their presence—past, present, or future. The older layers gave themselves away with their darker tones of brown, their moldy smell and wet heaviness. Under that carpet, augmented with the passing of each season, the deceased awaited with nervous anticipation the releasing scream of the archangel's horn, certain to be loud enough for them to hear regardless of how high the leafs and the years accumulated upon them.

I continued walking under the canopy of dense foliage that reduced the rain to a steady cold mist. Up and down the sloped grounds, kicking the top yellow and amber leafs, imagining the many caverns and crawl-ways that the slithering worms must be continually excavating in their endless labors of undoing the bodies of the dead. I carried on in this fashion for a long time, letting my feet sink into the leafs, all the while examining the names and dates on the faded stones. Once again, I felt as if I could continue walking as I was forever, without anyone missing me. There was no one else there and it seemed like days since I had last seen another living person, back at the train station. Although obviously wet, the brown and yellow mass below me looked like a large expanse of softness and tenderness, inviting to my tired eyes. I was tempted to lie down on the bed of leafs, if only for a brief moment.

Finally, just around the time when I thought I might give in to the rest offered at my feet, I found it. The stone I had been looking for was small and looked even smaller as part of it had sunk into the earth. In rather ornate cursive letters (which made me smile, I remember, for reasons unknown to me then or now), it read: "Abraham Kalmen Leip Frydman." And below, "b.1880 (?), Lublin, Poland — d. May 3, 1946, Philadelphia, Pennsylvania." Only half of the Star of David could be seen; the other half was buried underground. After a while, beginning to feel cold and wet from being out in the rain for so long, I left the daffodils I had brought next to the stone and turned around to make my way back under the steady drizzle.

Aquí, en el medio de la historia, no hay una máquina. Decir el medio es decir el centro, aunque ni uno ni el otro exista. Vos y yo sí, pero sin medio, sin centro. Y pronto una más. Sea como sea, aquí no se encuentra al escritor que nunca publicó su museo eterno, ni a la máquina que él construye cuando se muere su amada para que alguien, o algo, le hable en la oscuridad de las noches. Ni un irlandés ciego que escribe en el habla inconsciente de su hija loca, una lengua que es todas las lenguas, un río que es todos los ríos. Ni siquiera la invención de un cineasta en una isla desierta que se proyecta a sí mismo para que un futuro lector lo encuentre en un diario personal. Lo que sí hay, como siempre, es la competencia con los simulacros y el sueño recurrente de la casa vacía con las tías que toman mate en yidish. Vacía pero no abandonada, agregás vos o agrego yo para así introducir la importancia de la distinción.

Cuando digo costura no me refiero al tapiz de la creación. Vos siempre con la nave de los locos, se te ocurre decirme ahora, así nomás, después del café y yo agradezco el comentario, el brinco verbal, por la referencia aluvial y su articulación dentro de un voseo adoptado. Aunque aquí también—sentados uno frente al otro en la mesita de nuestra cocina boulderiana, en un boliche inventado entre valijas y diccionarios—se trata de fragmentos repartidos, casi mutilados, y el sentimiento falso del hombre que piensa que todavía tiene sus piernas después de la doble amputación. Lo único que sé de mi bisabuelo materno es que le amputaron una pierna, y después la otra, estaba tan viejito, el pobre zeide, así lo cuenta mi mamá, al zeide siempre le tocaba decir el *peisaj*, en yidish por supuesto, en el comedor del patio de la casa de Morelos, el pobre zeide, se quedó diabético, no me acuerdo bien, era chica yo, dice mi mamá. Y la cara, ¡ay!, su cara era increíble, esa piel como un cuero rubio grabado, arrugas tan profundas que parecían cortes de cuchillo, y sus manos grandotas y fuertes, como su voz, pero no duró mucho sin las piernas, el pobre. Le dijeron después del hecho que se las tuvieron que cortar, pero al principio, en el hospital e inclusive en su propia cama cuando lo trajeron devuelta, pensaba que se habían equivocado, que no se las habían cortado, porque todavía las sentía, estaba segurísimo de que todavía tenía las piernas; pero una vez que miró para abajo se dio cuenta que era verdad y chau, después de eso no duró mucho más, no lo mató la diabetes sino la doble amputación, eso es lo que siempre dijeron mis tías, explica mi mamá.

Un poco fuerte la metáfora, ¿no te parece?, insistís desde tu lado de la mesa, dejate un poco con la mutilación que esta no puede ser una historia de tortura: Uds. se fueron, no te olvides. Pero, ¿cómo más nombrar el hecho, el movimiento de los hechos? Como si se pudiera nombrar, como si para eso sirvieran las palabras, la maquinación del aparato. Tampoco me parece que se pueda volver a hablar con discos de jazz y blues en el extranjero, ni con un juego de chicas en el patio de un manicomio en Buenos Aires. Lo cual, de todos modos, ya está en el museo inédito y en la monstruosidad irlandesa, me hacés acordar rápidamente. No. Solamente la verdad, o la memoria de la verdad, que es lo mismo, no te rías, hasta que otro la rescriba, por supuesto. (*Mi piel también es cuero rubio...*) Sin pertenecer a los vencedores nos proponemos narrar la historia, eso sí. La mía, que se convertirá en la tuya y la tuya, que ya es la mía. (*... y mis manos también cortan como dagas.*) Donde estuve, perdido en los campos de maíz de Illinois. Es decir, antes de perderme, antes de perder, jugando en una placita de Belgrano todos los días al salir de la escuela. Con delantales blancos y libros de postes y piernas flaquitas corriendo a no dar más detrás de la esfera que irremediablemente gira hacia el norte. Pero no irremediablemente, sin remedio, porque sueño, con suerte, cuando no duermo, y si no hay una máquina como la mencionada, estás vos, y ya te estás yendo y yo, que hace mucho que ya me fui.

Como te habrás dado cuenta, está este otro idioma, en cartas, en el baúl, en recortes de diarios, un objeto arqueológico; el que una vez fue mi lengua y ahora abandono para recuperarlo. El alfabeto de la genealogía familiar y geográfica. ¿Aquí, en esta mesa querés armar el museo?, me preguntás desde enfrente, ¿al lado de las tazas y las cucharitas, entre el jarrito de leche y la mancha que no sale más? Porque vos sabés, agregás, que la mesa, por más que lo deseemos, no será nunca la oreja gigante que se imagina el escritor ciego en la taberna irlandesa, ni el receptor orgánico de una noche perpetua, ni el aparato polifacético del blanco nocturno del inmigrante italiano en una capital sudamericana. Más bien una máquina transformadora de historias, entre nosotros, tan constante como las consonantes entre las vocales de los idiomas de Europa del Este. En tus manos tranquilas, tan diferentes de las mías, sostenida por tus dedos largos y finos, la hoja contiene dos listas: de un lado los alimentos que necesitamos comprar en el supermercado, del otro la definición que acabás de sacar del diccionario. Y nuevamente me pregunto por la lengua, ahora en el centro, solo y con vos, cuánto que nos cuesta lo más simple, de la cocina a nuestro cuarto, en el coche y caminando, solo y con vos y un día con nuestra hija, qué carajo estoy pensando, si Uds. (y yo también, me dirás) están en otro idioma y ¿éste de quién es? (*Is this leaving not in English, after all...* ¡*Merde!*) Quisiera hablar el lenguaje de las memorias de mis viejos, de mis abuelos y así convertirme en ellas. Pero si no es mío: con las partidas y los años y las casas cambiadas, con aprender y olvidar, con estudiar y enseñar, con las idas y las vueltas, con vos: mi lengua ahora es una lengua de laboratorio. En seguida las ratas y el científico loco con el guardapolvo blanco, los monos y las jaulas en la isla perdida, devuelta el patio de la escuela y la sombra del gomero con las hojas caídas en las baldosas... Mas enseguida interrumpís: no te preocupes si la lengua es tuya o no, me advertís, el lenguaje no se posee, lo hemos dicho, es de todos, vos marcalo como puedas y marcate con él y chau, dejate de joder. Acordate lo que leímos ayer:

(*Yo no tengo la culpa que un señor ancestral, nacido vaya a saber en qué remota aldea de Polonia, se llamara...*)

Ni siquiera sé si la mesa es espejo o teléfono. Entonces no intentes traducir, contestás, para eso falta mucho, aunque toda escritura sea una reescritura, lo único importante, lo que queda después, es ser eficaz. Sólo me vacío de vísceras lingüísticas, no quiero analizar ni ser analizado, ni gratis ni a cien dólares la hora. Vos sos la que me enseñaste que lo más importante de la traducción es el ritmo, como en la cama, la distancia entre el *breathing* del hablante y el interlocutor. No te preocupes, a mí también me sorprende, aunque quizá no tendría que sorprender. Al revés, asombra que sea aquí solamente, ¿no? El río, el plateado, el único que conozco, será el más ancho del mundo, pero se ve que también corre profundo por estos lados. La aparición del castellano entre tantas partidas. *Leavings*. Con ele mayúscula, yéndose en un gerundio inglés, el irse, un proceso con principios inciertos, un azar sin determinismo y sin fin, hasta que nos alcance o el cansancio o la religión, la necesidad que impone el lenguaje mismo. Al igual que el devenir, el mero hecho de su inestabilidad requiere una resolución, agregás vos. Aunque sea artificial, aunque borre más que revele, el hecho es el mismo: marcar un pasado inexistente, crear un presente que deriva de ese pasado, dejar el futuro y la ciudad para otro, quien la armará nuevamente en la lengua en la que elija perseguirla.

Como si uno pudiera elegir lo natal, el sitio de compostura, la concepción o la partera por lo menos. *(¿Qué había en Concepción? En Concepción no había nada.)* El sabor de la torta de despedida, la sombra del gomero en el patio de la escuela, la respiración y el ritmo dentro de los cuales deben caer estas cláusulas: ¿cambia todo esto con la lengua como ocurre con la geografía? ¿No deberíamos pensar en términos geométricos? Devuelta con la física del viejo, che, ¿cuándo pasaremos de las matemáticas a las letras, *once and for all?* Antes de expiarlo para siempre, la tentación falsa de la confesión en tu familia, la absolución de transferirlo todo al presente, envolverlo en mi propio cuerpo, saber que viene de mí y termina en mí, mi cuerpo, el de ahora, el que mira a las montañas desde la cocinita de Colorado y se confunde más por la falta que implican que por el poniente que esconden. En inglés habría nuevamente un gerundio, en castellano surge el infinitivo. Marcar un comienzo, desde un centro ausente porque distante: antes de girar la página, abrir el deseo de una conclusión imposible, ir hacia la distancia para recrear la ausencia y ocuparla, en fin, *oh to settle down, to settle.* Y volver al otro idioma adoptado porque adaptado. Adaptar y adoptar: separación última inventada por la sustitución de una sola letra.

What about the other side, you ask, you started with your mother's line but left off with the promise of a city. And the child of a teacher trained across hemispheres. Tell me now about the Warsaw connection, tell me about the absent watchmaker in Villa Crespo and the philosophizing physicist in Orsay, for these too are the generations. Okay, but I am afraid that it is not much clearer on my father's side. Tailors and seamstresses should have been simple enough; now try stories about a jewel theft traveling between São Paolo and Colonia smuggling diamonds in dirty socks; about gambling debts so large it would take three lifetimes to pay them off; about remaining in poverty even after one's lottery numbers finally come up; about a counterfeiter from Warsaw who changes his name on the boat; about a half-brother (Jorge Naiman, my great half-uncle) who was ostracized from the family (by all except my father, who continued to surreptitiously watch soccer games with his favorite [half-]uncle every weekend) for marrying a Sephardic Jew—*la turca loca*, as they called her.

I will tell you what I know. My paternal grandfather—the watchmaker—is Isaac Itsic Weissmann in Yiddish, Isaac Alejandro Waisman in Spanish and Isaac Alexander Waisman in English. But he did not like Alejandro or Alexander and he thought that Isaac sounded too Hebraic, so he went by Ignacio Waisman. Ignacio died of pancreatic cancer in 1969 at the age of fifty-seven, knowing and not knowing what was killing him, since the family decided to keep the final diagnosis from him. He lies buried in La Tablada, in the outskirts of Buenos Aires. My own father turned fifty-seven last year.

My paternal grandmother is Jane Naiman Waisman in Yiddish, Chana Naiman Waisman in Polish and Juana

Naiman Waisman in Spanish. She at least does not have a middle name; Naiman is her maiden name. But she changed her first name to Ana—which is what she goes by here or in Argentina—because she did not like Juana, something about it sounding too much like the feminine of Juan. This is Bube Ana. Some twelve years after my Zeide Ignacio's death, Ana married Irving Jacob Grossman, a New York Jew who spoke Yiddish and English, but no Spanish. Ana's second marriage lasted just under two years.

And these are the lines and the names of the generations as we know them today.

But I don't really know the names and not just because the grandparents have changed languages so many times. For I have recently discovered that my last name is in all likelihood a relatively new invention. As you see, the pieces of the puzzle are incomplete and the final picture is unknown. What I have been able to ascertain is that my paternal great grandfather, my Zeide Ignacio's father—although he was, according to family stories, a reputable watchmaker—had some sort of shady business dealings involving stolen jewels in Warsaw between the World Wars and that, afraid of being detained, changed his name and sailed for South America in 1936. Supposedly, his name was Jaime Weinberg, which he changed to Weissman to facilitate his leaving. When he arrived in Argentina, the immigration clerk recorded his name as he heard it phonetically in Spanish, that is, as w-a-i-s-m-a-n. What I can say for sure is that before arriving in Argentina, the name of my paternal line was something other than Waisman (or Weissman, even). Somewhere between Warsaw and Buenos Aires, or perhaps after stepping off the boat, my last name came into existence. Traversing the entire Atlantic Ocean, changing continents, abandoning a thousand years of Ashkenazi history, crossing hemispheres and acquiring a new language with completely different syntactic and lexical roots was not enough: for whatever set of reasons, my great grandfather also found it necessary to take on a new name.

My mother organized a going-away party for me with my fourth grade teacher in Buenos Aires. We had the entire cafeteria just for our class, many kids brought presents (I especially remember a regulation-size soccer ball and a jersey from my favorite team, *River Plate*) and we ate *sandwiches de miga* instead of the usual bland spaghetti or stew that was served to us daily for lunch. My best friend Diego assured me that he would not let anyone ask Andrea, a cute brunette who I liked, out until I came back. (Some time in the third or fourth grade we had started imitating the older boys—who wore long pants and smoked cigarettes in the school's outer courtyard—by discussing the girls that we wanted to be with.) The teacher let us stay in the cafeteria most of the afternoon; we ate and made quite a mess, while she talked with my mother. For dessert we had an incredible chocolate hazelnut cake from the best bakery in Belgrano, each piece so tall you had to press it down with your hand to get it into your mouth. Everyone had a ring of chocolate around their mouths. I remember having a great time that day, especially so as it contrasted sharply with the solemn mood that had befallen our family and everyone I knew since March 24th. Although it was already getting cooler, after we ate we moved from the cafeteria to the inner courtyard, which was quickly transformed into an enclosed playground for the duration of the party, as games of tag and hopscotch and juggling my new soccer ball filled what was the otherwise serious daily setting.

We played as if we had all received gifts. The teacher seemed willing to give us the whole afternoon off; in fact, she barely paid attention to us and spent most of the time, instead, talking with my mother, the two of them removed from the group of us fourth graders. Although my parents had tried to explain it to me, I did not really understand why we were leaving; that is, I did not understand why we had to leave, while plenty of other people, plenty of other families, were finding ways to stay. Since we were having so much fun with the entire class and everything seemed fine right then, Diego and I went to ask my mom why I had to go. She looked at us, but did not answer. Instead, she put a hand on top of each of our heads, ran her fingers through our hair, bent down to give us a kiss and turned away. Then she walked off, past the venerable rubber tree in the courtyard and towards the doors that led to the principal's office. Diego and I stood immobile, in the middle of the school, looking after her, and though Diego soon jogged off to join the other kids playing with my new soccer ball, I stayed where I was, sensing something of relevance had just occurred, but unable to explain it to myself. A cool Fall breeze blew through the schoolyard, rustling the leafs of the rubber plant tree, creating unexpected vortices and eddies. I kept looking in the direction in which my mother had left even after she was gone. I kept looking. I knew that my mother was crying on the other side of the doors, for she always walked away like that when she was about to cry and did not want me to see her. I kept looking and imagined my mother crying alone on the other side of the closed doors.

Our first Christmas together you took me to the house where you grew up in San Luis Obispo. A world away even from where we met on 16th Street in San Francisco. (When I told you my name in Café Macondo you welcomed me to the beginning of the beginning of another hundred years.) From inside your old VW Thing, just past the Eucalyptus grove, you pointed out the sloped gravel driveway where your brother Craig put the station wagon in reverse and nearly ran over your father, who was getting groceries out from the back. He had to jump out of the way and chase the pale green car as it slowed into your neighbor's lot. And there, among the trashcans, he found the abandoned puppy, the basset hound-beagle mix, which you named Casey (the dog that grew up to eat apples on the back deck). In encroaching twilight we fought, a typical senseless holiday fight. I thought it had to do with going to midnight Mass with your family on Christmas and the fact that my family didn't celebrate Hanukkah when I was a child. We didn't even own a menorah, for that matter. And how difficult it was for me to fit in with a bigger and louder family. But you were not buying any of my explanations. Beyond the low stucco house was the open yard. I could not believe that there was no fence, just as you had told me. Remnants of the barn that burned down when you were a girl could be seen against a rising slope, its dark shadowy outline a skeletal figure against the impenetrable greens, yellows and browns of the shrubs and bushes around it. Chaparral green, I call it, you said, dry most of the year, then green and new with California poppies in early Spring, March. And the curves of a rich landscape of hills and valleys dotted with houses and the occasional raptor soaring between land and sky (red-tailed hawk, peregrine falcon, turkey vultures), a scene not man-made but also not entirely natural: *those who visit here are barely able to tell where the natural ends and the man-made begins.* And the air more translucent than it ever is in the city, creating an unmediated sensation. As if the scene required no translation.

(*Ghosts ascribed to places where you once were only confuse matters with their intractable lack of corroborating substance.*)

We forgot the fight for a moment, long enough to walk away from the car and take a look around. You showed me the pen where your father raised sheep. You talked about blind puppies and a horse that four of you rode at once. I have always liked your family, everyone I have met so far, anyway. I did not know what the fight was about back then. But you know now, you say. Still, you should have realized how foreign it was to me, to actually be there, to see the house in the middle of those green hills, the Eucalyptus grove on one side, the live oak trees on the other, the bittersweet fragrance all around us. Didn't you see me run my knuckles along the rough stucco walls of the house, feel the splintery wood of the shack with both my hands, peel a strip of bark from one of the oaks, play with a lump of dirt, crumpling it completely, throw small stones at the outlines of the burned-down barn? The idea of it: that we could be in front of that house—so plain and perfect—in which you grew up, see and touch it, smell the Eucalyptus mixed with the faint whiffs of the nearby farms, stand on the very lot where you lived your childhood. The fact that I could physically feel the corporeality of the house overshadow my elusive narratives of migration.

TEMPTATION

Our entire extended family came to Ezeiza Airport to see us off: there were dozens of people there, including second and third cousins who we only saw at major holidays or important anniversaries. But this was a major event and everyone came. It may have been as important for them to see this occurrence—to actually see us leaving Buenos Aires—as it was to say good-bye, but that did not matter then, nor does it now; family is unequivocally family at times like these. They gave us many going away presents. We were loaded: we had boxes of *alfajores* and jars of *dulce de leche*, and between my sister and I, we must have had five kilos of apple strudel that our grandmothers had made together. And one of my mother's aunts had baked an *onich lachech*; I still recall the light moist honey taste when we ate it three days later in New York. All this we managed to fit into numerous handbags. My mother even had several chunks of *provoletta* in her purse, somewhere near the tickets and the passports. Since it was an international flight, we arrived at the airport three hours prior to departure to check our luggage and our dog, which my sister and I refused to leave behind—and which my parents agreed to bring along, I realize now, as a conciliatory gesture. After dispatching the stuffed suit cases, the family trunk and the dog, we stood in the vast lobby on the ground floor open to the public, before the ticketed passengers went up an escalator and out of view into a small waiting room on the upper level of the airport to await boarding. Our family was there with us the whole time. Aunts and uncles took pictures of the four of us, then of my sister and I with our cousins. I remember sweat dripping from my father's hair line down onto his face. I remember my mother laughing and crying at the same time and repeating that we would be back in no time at all, in no time at all, she kept saying. Two cousins tried to get me to do my French accent and when I refused they retold the story of what I sounded like sitting with them in the back of the *colectivos* when we first moved back from France four years earlier. My uncle Nata (Natalio), who died of pancreatic cancer the year after we left, ran to buy my sister and I a bag of candy (*La vaca lechera*), although we were already loaded with all sorts of sweets and treats.

With all the flashes, food, gifts and hugs, it looked more like a party or someone's birthday—one of ours—than a sad event. The lobby at Ezeiza is very large; we stayed towards the center, near a row of seats, well away from the armed guards by the glass doors. From where we were gathered, I could see, throughout the spacious hall, other parties with their immediate and extended family and friends around them, much like us. For the most part the individuals did not stray beyond the groups where they were gathered, so that the lobby was comprised of these separate units, each numbering anywhere between fifteen and thirty individuals, each separated by an expanse of well-polished flooring below the tall ceilings. The groups, in this manner, resembled loosely-knit islands in a sea of marble, all self-contained, its members unwilling to drift outside their confines, unless someone had to rush to the restroom or hurry to buy food or drink. From the edge of our island I looked at the others; everyone seemed to be talking and hugging and kissing and crying at once. I could hear a few of the other groups, but separated as we were, the sounds that drifted towards me were like the strange clicks and clacks of another tongue, familiar yet foreign. On the outside of all of this, the soldiers standing at every entrance or exit, young and slim, appeared to be alternately sad and angry when they looked at us or at any of the other parties, clustered in their respective isles, who had come to see their loved ones depart. And it was all departures, for as far as I can remember there were no arrivals on that day, only leavings. The soldiers, meanwhile, held their machine guns stiffly at waist level. They all looked strikingly similar to each other and to my unusually quiet cousin Claudio, whose black hair was cropped short for the military service which he was to begin the week after we left.

I walked up and down Higuera Street in the rain looking for figs, past the one-story San Luis Obispo houses with their cars pulled up in the driveways, many of them four-wheel drive sports utility vehicles. The lawns sloped up from the street to the base of the houses, as there were no sidewalks there, but no traffic, either, not on a weekend like that, everyone was inside with that kind of rain. Lawns whose bright green, in contrast with the surrounding yellowish shrub canyons, belied all sense of nature, spoke of hours spent fertilizing, mowing, weeding, of thousands spent on sprinkler systems. A garden with planted tulips. The family with three children and seven cars. The retired teacher with the black cats. The doctor who has been having an affair for eight years with the woman who sings at the Patio Café across the street from the old Mission. The one-theatre movie house downtown. Puddles on the pavement and a small creek that a mother-in-law-to-be was calling a raging torrent.

I suppose I could live here, I remember thinking as I continued under the rain, as long as there was a café within walking distance, a place for coffee, people watching and space when the family tension became too much. A roomful of studying undergraduates, fogged-up windows, jeans and sweatshirts and I could be anywhere in the U.S. again, a new college town waiting for me when I finished my degree. Except, back out on Higuera Street, the water still coming down steady and hard (the sprinklers off today), I kept walking, searching, a moving semi-dry mushroom stalk under the umbrella. Live oak and beech trees, an occasional maple or pine along the streets and, beyond, manzanita bushes in the canyon chaparral. Whereas the Eucalyptus groves that separate one from the other remind one more of Australia than of the Mediterranean.

I always have a hard time with your family, there are so many of you, four brothers and sisters, nephews, nieces, cousins. The neighbor from Corralitos Street who comes over with the latest gossip and a platter of cold cuts. I am welcomed to such a degree that I disappear in the melee, before you say grace, before the quick meal. Again in translation. Cleaning up is my favorite part, the rain still falling outside, all weekend long, washing dishes with your father, hearing about his nearly forty years as a high school teacher, the changes that occurred when the children of the migrant workers started attending the school, something about the field workers' strike over the hills before that, but nothing about the angiogram or the procedure to insert the stent, even when I ask him about his health.

The next day you would take me to San Juan Capistrano, show me another of your missions as I looked for compatriots among the swallows. But that day, a language misplaced, misused, more evident at the intersection of California and Toro Streets, where all I saw were large cars and the enormous supermarket and the video store and the frozen yogurt shop and Thrifty Drugs behind the falling rain. Everything was gray this time around. The Safeway was bright and big, anything you might want, packaged and labeled, the only thing needed was to find the right aisle: grapes from Chile and melons from New Zealand, fresh cut meats and warm bread at the bakery. I aimed my cart for the frozen section, picked out a gallon of Dreyer's ice cream for dessert.

Outside again, I went down for a last look at the train tracks before I headed back, knowing you'd be waiting for me inside, on Cazadero and Conejo Streets, in the house where you'd grown up. I knew not to bother looking along Oso Street by now, that would be too much to ask for, but the figs, I thought the figs had a chance.

The conversation between the two is always the same. (They are like us, you say, they are us, you ask, but I do not have an answer to that question.) What does it take to be happy? Language, streets drawn by words. Which one is the daughter, the sister, the lover? *The nation is a linguistic concept*, a magnet of memories with gray skies and endless potholes. They talk in Buenos Aires, New York, before twenty-dollar phone calls in the middle of the night. They too sit at a table in a café, drink vermouth or espressos in an island outside time. *The unstable character of language defines life on the island.* How many times can one be expected to begin over again? New world, new hemisphere, new country, new language. New, new, new, new. Sic. East to west, south to north. How many professions unlearned, texts unread? Taylor, watchmaker, physicist, teacher. And now a composer, or a first fiddle dreamt for tomorrow. In her case a different shift, like the first snow of the season, as my mother's hair turned white overnight. Mine is also different, but in another sense, for a translator's shift is internal, as words become malleable: where bridges and mirrors once stood waters now promise to burst. *On the island they cannot picture, they cannot imagine, what is outside.*

There is an anxiety as strong as any religious belief that deifies the original and always prefers the source to the imitation, as if chronology could determine value. As if there was a single direction, a chart of identifiable moves that preconditioned how one is derived from the other. As if there were anything other than others, as if there were an original. This belief threatens not only lovers of the simulacra, but also those who are reproductions, and those, like us, who reside in between.

The topic is always the same, here or there. Take me by the hand, show me the walls, let us find the tracks leading to an empty house in a dream. *El tranvía y sus 20 poemas.* And the mother, you ask, where is she? You have told me that she, like my father, is the teacher, but that is not enough. *Language is as it is because it accumulates the remnants of the past with each generation and renews the memory of all the dead languages and all the lost ones.* There is more, then, even if we have to spend every day searching through a heap pile of recollections. I know that the syntax can cross over, that the contamination of one with the other is the best combination, even if the derivation remains undeterminable.

The translator finds an object that is part of a larger continent and that contains everything in its language up to that point in time. A living museum, an interactive photo album. A place that one can always visit, but which, once one has left, can never be one's home again. The translator visits as if he were an outsider, even if he once lived there, even if he grew up there and still on certain days considers its language his mother tongue.

In a way, it is another parenthesis. As is this: you and I at the kitchen table, again after so long, searching for words to bridge a space. Moments of movement that happen once, and, even as they are happening, one knows will never be the same again. Every move is one-way, you say, trying to reassure me from the other side. For example, a three-month journey across the Atlantic between the two Wars. A flight over the Equator, clutching a soccer ball in a boy's unstable sleep. A drive from New York to Illinois to San Diego in a Ford Fairmont station wagon, imported mutt and jar-full of crickets in the back. A U-haul pulled across the continental US, heading west again. Or how to go from a yard near a Eucalyptus grove (a flat three-bedroom house in English, a junk drawer in a dream), to a patio with aunts sipping *mate* and eating *pretzelech* in Spanish and Yiddish, via men drinking their daily short glass of whiskey in the living room, grimacing behind goatees.

Certain things never change. The home in which I always dream. The second person conjugation that feels like a caress, a warmth yearning to emerge, to jump around as if it were another game of hopscotch. You and I in bed.

Soon, very soon after we left, we began to turn our experiences into stories. That is how we were able to relate what we had just lived. But then, with time, the stories were all that remained. The experience was lost. Or so the story goes.

But if a sentence is a formula, as you maintain, then I am closer to my father than I had previously thought. And he to his, you quickly add. (The watchmaker: the physicist: the translator. Next: the violinist.) If writing is not entirely in our mother tongue, nor entirely in a foreign one, but always in both (as in others) in tension, then you and I are interchangeable, at least for the duration of this dialogue (the love rendered by the words), at least until our daughter comes to disagree. If her music is another language, fine fingers sliding on the neck of her perfect violin, then she may come to speak for all of us yet, as in the madwoman's soliloquy, as in the promise of the island surrounded by all the rivers of the world, frequented by lost socialists singing along to the melody of a half-forgotten song. Can the translator be blamed for copying the original?

The watchmaker is not in today; his son is covering the shop for him, although he knows almost nothing about his father's trade. It has always been a mystery to him, the shop and the work, his father's job and what his days are like. His father always left home before his children finished having breakfast, kissed his two boys on top of their heads, lifted his two girls and hugged them in the air. I'm going to the shop, I have timepieces to fix, is what his family heard him say every morning while they were still half-asleep, and off he would go for the entire day, not come back until after 10 PM on most days, after they had already had dinner, and even later on others. And then there were the arguments between the father and the mother, she screaming at him when he left, greeting him with more screams when he returned at night. And the two sons, always fighting when they should be getting ready for school, while the oldest daughter played with the youngest, a baby girl, as if she were the mother.

But today was different. You're coming with me, he had said to him during breakfast, you can go to the afternoon session of school straight from the shop. His mother had argued, the usual phrases and raised voices, plus the theft of one of her children on this day, but to no avail. After they had made it out of the family fray, father and son walked together in complete silence, the serious mood of the city streets at that time of morning reflected on the father's face, and in turn imitated by the son, for exactly four long blocks down Avenida Warnes, then left on Malabia for three shorter ones further, at which point they stopped at a corner, one block before Avenida Corrientes. The boy had been to his father's shop only once before, and that long ago, when he was much younger. This time, he did not see it at first, and could not even tell there was a storefront where they were standing. The entrance was a small door nearly hidden against the wall of a tall building. You're covering the shop this morning, son. I'll check back periodically. If anyone comes for a pick-up, just tell them I'll be back in the afternoon. If they want to leave something, fill out one of these. He showed him the order forms, and the tags to attach to each piece to be repaired. Whatever you do, don't give anyone anything, and don't leave the shop, okay? There shouldn't be too many customers anyway. Most of them come after lunch. I'll be back soon.

Now the watchmaker's son—the eleven-year old who has never been on vacation, has never been outside Buenos Aires, not even to the Tigre Delta; who has spent the majority of his life in the vicinity of his neighborhood, between Chacarita and Villa Crespo—stands inside the shop that is more a kiosk stuck into a wall than an actual store. His first time there since that initial visit, five or six years ago, he could not remember exactly, when he had been brought there with his brother and sisters by their mother to see their father's new shop. Smaller than he remembered, it is even more spectacular in a sense, for no space is wasted—the tight room is filled with old clocks hanging on every centimeter of wall space, mechanisms and various parts and tools piled everywhere in boxes opened and closed (the boy does not know their names, but is sure that if his father were there he could tell him what each one was called), and a crowded workbench beyond which is the window looking out at the street.

He stands next to the tall stool, does not dare to climb up and sit on it yet. His father's high stool and workbench. The stool comes up to his chest, the workbench nearly above his head—the watchmaker's son is short and heavy—and he feels dwarfed inside the shop even though his father must feel like a giant in there. It is a strange magical place, with all the clocks on the walls stopped at different hours and none of them working, as if time had ceased to run in a thousand different imaginary countries, in different time zones, at a different time in each. And the radio, mounted on the wall opposite the window, the source of the old tangos his father sings to himself when he is home, as if he were still there, in the shop, working and listening and singing along, always a raspy longing in his low voice.

The watchmaker's son does not want to sit down. He would rather stand there and imagine his father sitting on the high stool, legs bent under him and resting on the bar, large upper body stooped over the workbench, a white rectangle of light coming in through the window facing the street, concentrating with his gray-green eyes, broad eyebrows and thick set of hair, holding a silver pocket watch in his left hand and a thin screwdriver in his right (the watchmaker's son is sure that it must have a special name, this fine-tipped screwdriver, and the other tools his father uses, only he doesn't know them). He imagines his father performing an operation on the graceful instrument of time that is as precise as surgery. He can almost hear his father singing along to the music from the radio now, like he does in the morning before he leaves for work, when everyone else is still getting up, humming under his breath (*Soy hijo de Buenos Aires, por apodo 'El Porteñito', el criollo más compadrito, que en esta tierra nació*) as he manipulates the mechanism under the face of the timepiece (What is that screwdriver called—if he only knew!), the tiny wheels and gears usually out of sight revealed to his father like a patient's insides to a surgeon.

A man cannot function in this society without a good watch, his father always says, it is as important as having a strong heart and a bit of luck on your side. Every kitchen should have a clock on its wall, everyone needs an alarm clock next to his bed, and every man should have a watch in his chest pocket. Repairing clocks is like keeping time going. The whole country—the whole world—would come to a screeching halt if there were no watchmakers like me, it would be like a man without his own heart, the youth imagines his father thinking as he adjusts a minute screw with that tool (What could its name be, good God?!), then closes the face back over the naked mechanisms, winds the gear, and looks on as the second hand starts to tick on the face of the watch inside the silver casing.

He looks up, past the workbench and through the small window into the street, observes the people hurrying down Malabia towards the corner of Corrientes and the entrance to the subway. Line B, from Federico Lacroze all the way downtown and on to the port at Leandro N. Alem, the boy says to himself. It must be eighty-five meters from his father's shop (the watchmaker's son likes to estimate distances like this, to be able to measure the world and oneself in it in concrete terms). The people are well-dressed, mostly men in dark suits and jackets, ties, leather shoes and briefcases, and some women in secretary skirts and stockings, their hair pulled back or tied up, heels shaping the curve of their ankles and calves. Looking out, the boy wonders how many of those men have pocket watches; all the fancier-dressed ones do, he is sure. They would not be going about their day so seriously, he says to himself, if they did not have time tucked inside their suit pockets, they would lose track of everything, they would constantly have to stop and ask somebody what time it was, losing precious seconds and minutes in the process. And the ladies with their slender wrist watches, almost like bracelets (women's wrists and ankles so much more delicate than men's)—although he did not see too many of these in his father's shop, he was not sure why, still he was certain the women, too, would bring their watches there if they broke down, they could not afford to be without a watch either, especially if they worked outside the home—unlike his mother, who was always home, when he left in the morning, when he came back for lunch, when he came home after school. His father's shop so perfectly located, right in front of all those people, where they could drop off their watches if they broke down, get them fixed before they lost too much time without them. As I have always thought, the watchmaker's son thinks, you have to have a timepiece not just to know what time it is, but to actually *have* time. Without a watch or a clock, you are lost, timeless, wandering aimlessly without direction. You are stuck in a past that no longer exists without any chance of recovering your present and your future.

The eleven-year old turns back to the tall stool, decides he is going to try to sit on it. If he is going to be there, to occupy the space his father usually occupies, even if it is only temporarily, for a couple of hours or so while he takes care of some business around the corner, as his father said before leaving him there alone, then he might as well do it in style. Act like he imagines his father would (without breaking anything, of course). So he reaches up to the wall behind him and turns on the radio. Already tuned to the right station, a tango blares out mid-song from among all the different frozen times on the wall next to it. Then he turns back around and begins the climb onto his father's chair. He thinks it is going to be difficult, him being only a boy still, really (but into the second decade of his life, he likes to tell himself), and a bit on the heavy side at that (so much more like his mother physically than like his father; but at least he has his father's eyes and hair, he thinks to himself). He manages to jump right up, however, (I must be getting more agile, he thinks), and before he knows it he is sitting on the tall stool, his legs under him, his elbows on the large work bench, the rectangle of light from the window right in front of him, the music filling the shop from behind him. (*No hay ninguno que me iguale, para enamorar mujeres, puro hablar de pareceres, puro filo y nada más.*) The tango comes in scratched, the song sounding not as if it came from a meter behind him (the distance the boy estimates), but rather from far away—or from one of the many times on the broken clocks hanging on the wall, he thinks.

He looks out the window at the street from a different perspective now, sitting on the tall stool, higher up, more clear. This is how my father must see things, he says to himself, and tries to hum along to the song, not because he knows the tune, but because he is certain that that is what his father would be doing. Then he reaches down, grabs an old pocket watch from a box under the table, with the casing broken off and only one hand left. From the tool set on the table he takes a very thin delicate screwdriver (it is the one he was wondering about before, only now he does not care so much what its name might be), and acts as if he is about to fix the watch. Just like my father, he says to himself, staring at the broken timepiece in his fat little hand, and begins to cry.

To measure time (even before the invention of digital). To contain it in a hand-held device, to situate it in the wheels and gears of a man-made mechanism (or the combinations of zeros and ones in a chip smaller than a fingernail). In Cortázar's story "The Pursuer," Johnny, a jazz musician based loosely on Charlie Parker, notices the deceiving nature of time while riding the metro in Paris. He realizes that in the distance between any two stops he can fully experience an event that lasts much longer than the train ride itself. He can relive a childhood memory and every note of a fifteen-minute song ("Save it, Pretty Mama"), for example, in the span of ninety seconds—all the while conscious of the fact that he is still on the metro, living both experiences simultaneously. This realization ultimately destroys him.

Boarding took place so quickly that I barely realized the moment of leaving had actually occurred. Today I wonder if there actually was a specific identifiable moment of leaving, if that is something that can be extrapolated from time, from memory, and if I, in all the excitement, being young and confused, somehow missed it—missed precisely the moment for which I am now searching. There were many hugs and kisses and tears; I remember it still seemed like it might have been a celebration instead of a farewell. Then, before I knew it, we were on the plane, the four of us, our bags stuffed with clothes, toiletries and all the presents of food, crowded in and surrounded by strangers, everyone trying to find a place for their belongings. We were on that plane—a large 747—in the center row of seats for a long time before it finally took off. It was smoky and the passengers paced up and down the aisles nervously throughout the flight. I expected to start hearing English right away, but everyone still spoke Spanish. If that flight was representative at all, then South Americans, and Argentines in particular, are certainly a restless people.

It was very cramped, even once the plane took flight, as if there were more passengers than seats, and clearly more bags than room for the bags. People were up and about and soon I started wandering around as well. A little later, I took out the new soccer ball that my friends from school had given me and started to juggle in the aisles. It was after a meal and the stewardesses must have been taking a break or working in the back, because no one told me to stop. My parents were tired and seemed content to let me go, as long as I was entertaining myself. I juggled with my feet and head, with my shoulders and thighs, up and down the aisles, not letting the ball touch the ground, thinking that if it did, it would go right through the floor of the plane and fall thousands of meters to the earth below. My muscles felt light and free, as if the tight quarters inside the airplane actually helped to improve my ball-handling skills. And if the ball did get away, passengers would kick or head it back to me from their seats. I had just about everyone in on it, it was great fun. It helped to pass the time; we were all keeping the ball in the air, even as we ourselves were kept airborne by the flying machine. People oohd and aahd with the various bounces of the ball, breathing a sigh of relief when it was once again under control, saved either by myself or some friendly co-passenger, who, remembering moves from his youth, would stretch far out from his seat and tap the ball back to me with the side of a foot, displaying his fine leather shoes in the process, as if amorously caressing the sphere, willing it to stay afloat.

After a while, I began to feel very tired and went back to my seat. I must have fallen asleep. I remember being upset because I wanted to be awake when we crossed the Equator, to see if I could feel or see any change. But when I woke up we were already descending and now I did finally hear English, in the form of distorted noises that must have come from the pilot in the cockpit, although no one could decipher what he was saying. When we reached New York, before disembarking, I went to look for my soccer ball, to make sure I still had it. It was there, in the overhead bin, next to the apple strudel and the *provoletta*, but it had deflated—perhaps from the change in altitude, or latitude?—all the way down to its leather core. It was so much smaller than it had been, almost insignificant now, but there was no time to complain: we were quickly gathering everything and getting off the plane. No one seemed to notice what had happened. I clasped what had become by then nothing but a little toy ball tightly under my arm as we walked towards customs.

This kaleidoscope of shapes suggests objects that threaten us with cold edges and points, multifaceted sides and discontinuous viewpoints. Hidden are the items we seek—a violin and a picture, perhaps; or at least what they have to offer: music, space, as in a room where all of this can happen. A hand on the small of a woman's back. Or the many ways to quench a thirst: poured hot, passed around through the years, drawing circles with dissipating steam and loose strands of conversation. Or an old woman leaning over a sewing machine, bobbin spinning, joining pieces of fabric into a grandson's pair of pants, foot peddle pumping to the sounds of kids shouting outside. A shaded patio where aunts drink *mate* in summer and gossip in Yiddish, Spanish. My grandparent's shop in front of their apartment, or house, the wicker basket under the ironing table filled with pins and needles, thistles and threads, buttons, measuring tapes. The side window where I stand, unraveled, behind textured glass. Before you and me there was this. A cousin's swaying hips.

Or maybe a pipe, dropped among a stack of books, their titles obscured by dust and ashes, grays and ambers. The man looks for his pipe behind the grand piano, inside his leather shoes, resting along the windowsill. The rain blowing outside, driving always towards an entrance. Preparing for an evening at the theater and a late dinner of fresh salmon. Slender fingers deliberate through minor scales, finding notes fine as diamond dust, tense, sliding to release delicate vibratos. Hundreds of feet shuffling to the movements of chamber music. Or a walk towards the wharf of a silver river wide as an ocean. Even as all fragment into an increasing number of planes and I find myself once again sifting through voices, strings and clothing. A violin and a picture.

El zorzal—as the saying goes—sings better every day. The journey from the moment of his mysterious death in a plane crash in Medellín, Colombia (he had vowed that he would never fly in an airplane) on June 24, 1935, until his remains were laid to rest in the Artist's Pantheon of Chacarita Cemetery in Buenos Aires was as fantastic as his short but legendary career.

> *Verás que todo es mentira,*
> *verás que nada es amor*
> *que al mundo nada le importa*
> > *Yira, yira,*
> *aunque te quiebre la vida,*
> *aunque te muerda un dolor,*
> *no esperés nunca una ayuda,*
> *ni una mano, ni un favor.*

As news of his death spread, the Americas fell into mourning. The newspapers said that there were at least three suicides in Buenos Aires. In La Habana, a girl was found dead in her room, the walls postered with pictures of Carlos Gardel; others were rushed to the hospital just in time. There was a huge memorial gathering at the Teatro Esmeralda in Santiago de Chile. Radio stations ceased playing tangos for a week, then played all of his compositions around the clock for months. A notice above the entrance of the Teatro Liceo in Buenos Aires read: *Silencio. Carlos Gardel ha muerto.* The racetracks closed that Sunday, in part out of respect for one of Gardel's favorite obsessions. Cinemas showed his seven movies at half-price admission. The leading headline of *La Prensa* read: *¡Qué triste se queda sin vos Buenos Aires!*

Following an argument regarding his native land between Uruguay and Argentina (few people knew that Gardel had actually been born in Toulouse, France) for the repatriation of his remains, his mother Doña Berta intervened to avoid a potentially touchy situation and declared that he should be buried in Buenos Aires. Thus, on December 17, 1935, Gardel's body was removed from San Pedro Cemetery in Medellín; the coffin traveled through the jungles of the northern regions of the Amazon and across the Andes by rail (on some of the more precipitous mountain roads, it had to be carried on men's shoulders, as the train swayed through the high passes) to the Pacific Colombian port town of Buenaventura, where he was loaded on to a ship that sailed to Panamá, through the Panamá Canal, and up to New York City. He stayed there for one week at the Funeraria Hernández on West 114th Street so that New York's Latin district could pay its respects.

From Harlem he was taken back to Pier 48 and loaded onto the *SS Pan America*, en route to Argentina. On January 31, 1936 the ship docked at Rio de Janeiro, where Brazilian delegations filed on board with floral tributes. On the morning of February 4th, the ship pulled into Montevideo; the coffin was taken ashore and placed in the central arcade of the customs building, whose walls had been covered with black velvet tapestries for a short lying-in-state in an improvised catafalque. Thousands of *montevideanos* filed by to pay tribute as the band of the local fire brigade played funereal music. Finally, a flower-festooned truck took the coffin back to the quayside and a crane hoisted it back on board the liner. Sometime past midnight, the ship weighed anchor and moved out into the smooth waters of the Río de la Plata.

Canción maleva, lamento de amargura,
sonrisa de esperanza, sollozo de pasión,
este es el tango, canción de Buenos Aires,

*nacido en el suburbio, que hoy reina en todo
el mundo.*

Around midmorning on February 5th, the *SS Pan
America* eased into the north dock of the port of Buenos Aires with Gardel's coffin. Some twenty to thirty thousand
people had gathered to welcome *el zorzal*. Old and young
women held hand-sewn handkerchiefs to their faces as they
leaned against each other and stood on their toes to see him
carried out; young men climbed atop railroad cars at the nearby
Retiro terminal for a better view as a crane placed the crate
on the quayside. Mounted police had to hold people back so
that the hearse could move out. The rain of flowers began to
descend upon it as it made its way to the indoor arena of
Luna Park. Once inside, the coffin was placed next to a large
silver crucifix in the center of the arena, where the boxing
ring usually stood. *El zorzal* rested there with even more make
up than usual on his doll-like face.

* * *

Arc lights covered in black crêpe shone down on Gardel's
coffin lying next to the three-meters-tall silver crucifix. A
procession of people walked in between wreaths arranged in
double rows to either side of the catafalque. Tall candles
showed the way and here too flowers grew into mountains.
Women cried like babies in need of nursing as they waited
their turn in line. The homage inside the Luna Park arena
lasted from noon on February 5th until the following morning,
when the coffin was loaded onto a funeral carriage and the
procession towards the cemetery began.

*Siento llorar, compadre, el corazón,
al regresar al barrio en que nací,
al recordar mis años de purrete—*

mi madrecita, mi hogar, todo perdí.
Recuerdo mi lejana juventud
que iluminara el sol de la ilusión,
cuando un gotán nos transportaba al cielo...

Preceded by several coaches already loaded with flowers, the funeral carriage set off up Avenida Corrientes to traverse the seventy blocks bisecting Buenos Aires. With the radiant immovable sun perched high above, the cortège made its way through downtown, crossed Calle Florida with its many restaurants and cinemas and went through the heart of the theater district. Small bands at street corners and on the sidewalks in front of his favorite cafés played tangos from Gardel's repertoire, as well as other popular songs, and occasionally the national anthem. Three kilometers away from Luna Park, the multitude accompanying the entourage extended at least ten city blocks behind it. Half way to the cemetery, the funereal carriage was joined by traditionally attired horsemen from the Leales y Pampeanos Gaucho Center of Avellaneda, and a few blocks later, by an old-fashioned ox-cart containing members of a theater company dressed as gauchos. In addition to the thousands now in the procession, thousands more watched the slow progress by leaning out the windows and balconies of the tall apartment buildings that flanked the width of Avenida Corrientes. From these heights the people continued the rain of flowers which had begun the day before at the port. It was hot; colorful blossoms drifted down from the highest buildings to land on the throngs on the wide avenue below, creating a bright shimmering atmosphere.

Mi Buenos Aires querido,
cuando yo te vuelva a ver,
no habrá más penas ni olvido...

Hoy que la suerte quiere que te vuelva a ver
ciudad porteña de mi único querer,
oigo la queja de un bandoneón,
dentro del pecho pide rienda el corazón.

Hours later, as the procession arrived at its destination, an additional thirty to forty thousand people had to be cleared out from Chacarita Cemetery before the coffin could be brought in. It was finally placed in the chapel of the Artist's Pantheon, outside of which stood a bronze statue of a smiling dinner-jacketed Gardel in one of his jaunty confident poses, his hair slicked back, the features of his face fine and perfect, a lighted cigarette in his right hand. The statue has become known as the smiling bronze. Ever since, Gardel recordings have been played daily for at least one hour on Buenos Aires radio stations. And at the end of this recurring tribute, the announcer says what is said each and every day since Gardel's death, and what everyone knows is true about *el zorzal*: that he sings better every day.

It is just your mother and I out here now, sitting at the dining room table over a game of Yatzhee. You have all gone to the den to watch a movie on TV. Score cards and number two pencils at our side, the cup with the dice between us, Mildred explains the rules to me in a serious tone that suddenly makes me feel worried. She has a large plastic mug full of ice and diet Dr. Pepper by her right hand, which she slurps from compulsively when I take my turn; then, when it's her turn, she slides it aside, rolls, adds up her points and quickly fills in the score card. I look at the miniature ceramic doll collection and the fragranced candles atop the oak silverware dresser against the flowered wall that separates me from the den and, although I get details from Mildred, who's caught me glancing in that direction, about when and where the various pieces were purchased (the silverware a wedding present from her mother, circa 1956; the dolls from Texas and Florida, before the kids were born; the wallpaper put up in the summer of 1985, the year you went away to college), despite these specific dates, the overall impression of the wall, as of the entire house, is that it has always been neatly organized and decorated for some holiday or another, as it is now.

As our game of Yatzhee progresses, other topics of conversation, besides the house and its history, include tomorrow's plans (a drive to Hearst Castle), the work scheduled for the deck next summer (to be followed by a new gate around the front yard the following year), something about doughnuts after church every Sunday when you were children and stories of board games with the Christian cousins on some past occasion that I have apparently missed. With an unexpected Full House on her last roll, Mildred defeats me in Game #1. She goes briefly to the kitchen to get us each a large bowl of peach cobbler and vanilla ice cream, rushes back to refill her mug with ice and diet soda and hurries back to the dice.

* * *

The strong hand flips the cup over, dice and cup smash against the wooden table, the cup is quickly lifted away, the numbers on the five cubes revealed momentarily before they are swept off the edge of the table and the cup is set back with its five dice ready for the next player's turn. It all happens in a flash, the only pause that of the five dice with their telling black holes before their disappearance into the cup again. Like the click of a hand on the grandfather clock in your parents' living room. The motion is fast and natural, no one interrupts their smoking or drinking or talking when it takes place, but everyone's eyes focus on the five dice for that one instant when movement stops and the numbers are revealed. Ignacio inhales the smoke from his non-filtered cigarette compulsively while he waits his turn. Topics of conversation include the results from last weekend's soccer matches, the stifling heat in the city during the long summer and a discussion about how the tango is becoming popular in France. No one talks about the numbers, however, about who the lucky fellow might be who had won the lottery this week, although this is usually a preferred item of speculation among the men in the café.

* * *

Your family's house, as it turns out, is a patchwork of home repairs, the new linoleum floor in the kitchen, the swinging side door for the cat and dog, the water-saving devices in the bathroom, the refurnished den (its walls lined with mounted photographs of the children at all ages), the home entertainment center your father built in the garage. Your parents made babies and stretched the house out with each one of you. Mike the cat lives in the bathroom, likes to join you when you take a shower, licks the drops of water off the cold tiles after you are done, then jumps back to the cabinet and falls asleep on a stack of fluffed beach towels. Wears a bell on his collar to prevent him from catching birds and dragging them back into the house half-dead. Flash the English bulldog looks fierce (he will frighten the grandkids in the future, I'm afraid) but he is really sixty pounds of pusillanimous muscle (he'll turn out to be great with children, taking abuse to no end with no reaction whatsoever). His teeth stick out in odd directions and he falls asleep at random places in the house and begins to snore. Takes a flatulence pill every morning in a tablespoon of peanut butter. Sleeps on a pile of pillows in a corner of your parents' bedroom.

* * *

Ignacio blows smoke toward the overhead fan. The fan spins above the game of La Generala, barely stirring the stale air, slicing the slanted morning sunlight of the tables near the windows facing Calle Malabia. The large espresso machine behind the bar releases steam and the sound makes Ignacio think of traveling, of leaving on a steamer to Brazil or Italy, the sun and the beaches of Rio, the avenues and the bars of Milan, of being somewhere where no one knows him, where no one can talk to him because the language is different, fancy and romantic, and he is alone to do whatever he wants. A place without wives, without a shop that never brings in any money, without sons who can only cover his shop for so long, without daughters who grow up only to start their own families with other men. The fan spins and seems to slow down for a moment. As he looks up Ignacio cannot help but see the image of a watch face superimposed upon it, the fan spinning, splicing time, a giant clock ticking above his head, above him and his friends and their game of dice, marking time and always the same time, an empty spinning overhead. And those numbers he had played his entire life, those numbers he had meant to play every week of his life until they finally came up or he died, whichever came first.

* * *

The cobbler is amazing, with fresh peaches, thick syrup and homemade crust, and the vanilla bean ice cream providing the ideal contrast in taste and temperature. Mildred talks faster with each roll of the dice, keeps drinking the diet soda and talking and playing faster and even though she tells me what I should do with my rolls, her dice are always better, the right combinations come up at the right time for her, when she lifts the cup it is always the number she needs to fill in another high-scoring box. Game after game she takes the lead and then easily, almost apologetically, completely destroys me. I start to wonder what movie you have found, why it is so quiet in the den, how long Yatzhee games last. Meanwhile, Mildred grows with each roll of the dice, she slides her chair forward, her face and shoulders and arms come closer to me as she rolls again, four sixes she gets this time, laughs an expansive laugh, her mouth broadens more than I had thought possible, her eyes widen, her hands reach for the cup and the dice and she rolls and gets Yatzhee and drinks more soda and I am dwarfed as I sit across this woman who bore and raised you in this here house.

* * *

Every combination of the dice remind him of his numbers that day. He knows he is going to lose the Generala that morning but does not really care. He has already lost, lost with his own numbers. Now it is all over. The same numbers never come up twice, everyone knows that, you play the same numbers every week of your life hoping they come up once, just once, dreaming of everything you have never been able to have, hoping they come up just once. A trip to Brazil or Europe, with the whole family even. You hope they come up once. But not twice. Once those numbers come up once it is all over. Next week will be some other sucker's lucky day, not his. Not his ever. He does not really blame his son for what he did, does not blame anyone. It's just the way the dice fall, as he always says, just roll and see what happens.

For several years now his oldest son had been saving the money for the lottery ticket instead of following his father's careful instructions of which numbers to buy. Giving it to his mother, as he claimed, or keeping it for himself, it did not matter so much anyway, Ignacio would have done the same thing and he knows it. What's the use of playing the same numbers every week, what's the use, except that those number might come up one time, and then, and then. What's the use, that's what Ignacio wants to know, what's the use. He grabs the cup, flips it over, lifts it up and there they are again, his numbers, all scrambled and saying to him: that's just the way we fell today.

I remember very little of our 1976 arrival. I know we left in late May, that it had been starting to get cool in Argentina (the onset of Autumn in the gusts of wind blowing in the school's courtyard) and that the muggy heat of New York, especially when we got into July, came as quite a shock: for some reason we did not have quite the right clothing, my parents had gotten confused and at the last minute had shipped the summer and spring clothes in the large trunk that reached us months later, and had brought our winter ware in our overstuffed suitcases with us instead. I remember very little of that winter become summer. Although I can still see our Argentine mutt all doped up, slipping on the waxed floors and pissing all over the lobby of Kennedy International Airport when we first landed in New York after spending thirty hours with the luggage, I don't remember what we did with our dog, for example, for the rest of that summer. I don't remember the apartment where we stayed for three months (apparently a tiny place in Queens owned by a chemist who my father knew from graduate school). I don't remember what my sister and I did all day (we must have spent it with my grandparents) while our father went out to look for work and our mother went to the diner where she waitressed (it would take her another two years to get her credentials validated in the U.S. and be able to teach high school again), learning new vocabulary such as eggs over-easy and a large plate of hotcakes. I don't remember the move from there to Champaign/Urbana in late August. I was ten years old. There are no pictures in the family albums from this period in our lives.

What about baseball, didn't you learn to play baseball in New York, you ask, as interested in arrivals as I am in departures. Yes, there was baseball, that I remember, except it wasn't baseball and I didn't quite learn it, either. It was stickball, the kids who played it called it stickball because you hit the ball, this small dark blue rubber ball, with a stick, like a broomstick without the broom on the end. That I remember, I remember holding the stick in my hand and never being able to hit the little blue ball, it would bounce off the wall behind me (in lieu of a catcher, I later realized) and back to the copper-haired boy who seemed much too thin to be able to throw that fast. The only time that I remember hitting the ball, I ran around the bases (drawn on the cement with chalk), but it was in vain: some kid had already caught my soft pop-up and I did not realize that I was out.

I wonder when, exactly, and where, I played this game. And what did my sister do while I was playing (trying to play) stickball? I have the impression that she stayed with me that entire summer, just as I had been in charge when we were even smaller in France, but this can't be right. Perhaps she went to some sort of day camp, or had a baby-sitter? I don't remember. And I somehow figured out how to play stickball, or at least was able to follow the instructions of the kids who were playing, because the instructions were told to me in Spanish, or in something that sounded like Spanish but was like nothing I had ever heard. The accents were all wrong, the slang didn't make any sense, the conjugations were a bit off—mine, that is, for I was definitely the foreigner there. Still, they let me play and yelled at me until I understood at least enough to stand in right field. But stickball remained as big a mystery to me as the kids who played it. I thought I knew geography so well, I could locate all the Argentine provinces and major rivers and other natural formations on a map, but I couldn't tell Puerto Rico from the Dominican Republic from any of the other islands in the Caribbean. I thought I knew so much about the world (Buenos Aires, France as a little boy), but I didn't even realize, until that moment, that there was more than one kind of Spanish in the world. I only knew one set of rules when we arrived in New York (*fútbol*) and one system of linguistic codes (*castellano*). It's not just that everything was different, that's a given. It's that there were no equivalences. N was no more a reflection of S than you are a reflection of me. For what kind of translation is needed to move a green city park in Belgrano to a charcoal cul-de-sac in Queens? Or the skill of feet to the eye-hand coordination needed to catch a rubber ball line drive?

You're right, arriving is no piece of cake either, even if (except when?) you are there to say welcome home. A South American seaport where family names are forever distorted, the hard smile of a French schoolmistress, a one-room house and tailor's shop in Villa Crespo, in the Bronx, in Hollywood, Florida, the snow, ice and maize of the Midwest, the deafening silence of a Southern Californian suburb, a spelling bee, the national anthem, the back seat of a VW Thing, the green outside a moving Honda, the hills behind a Central Coast house, an imagined flat in Noe Valley, the view from its bay windows, the view of snowed peaks blocking a new departure, a new arrival, another leaving. And eventually a third. But I do remember the flavor of that going-away cake and the rubber plant leafs fluttering at the base of our tree in the school's inner patio. I do.

Temptation may very well be the figure of the blue Chevrolet in the woman's gloved hand held high above the metropolis. The aimless gentleman with a hat barely in the frame, the threatening mutts and slinking cats at ground level (*planta baja*), stairwells descending or ascending, subways implied, skyscrapers suggested. Growls of fear from an elderly couple in brown raincoats, brown and gray throughout with streaks of red and splotches of green here and there, on Rita Hayworth's face (on the billboard advertising the latest [sic] movie, reflected in the night sky), on the patterns of bricks and shingles, on the glitter off the sequin. The search for reason in a madwoman's soliloquy. Again the memory of the grandmother, again the mask of the fabric. And always the outline of the faces of the boys (no possessive here), on the vast thighs of the *copera*, plumed hair dew and knee-high boots, in the bar near the port where men play *la generala* and alternate Vermouth with espresso. Waiting for the *colectivo* or the *tranvía* or the horse cart to come around the corner, for the airplane to gain altitude, for the dice to fall from leather tumbler to wooden table, for the number on the wheel to send the couple back home. The telephone starts ringing in the middle of the night, as reliable as a pocket watch recently adjusted with a miniature screwdriver. Waiting for thighs to shift, for a sign of life in any code—white lips not quite laughing above, in a city my ghost conpenetrates and concenters without me.

To speak a language in which the fine line between past and memory, between memory and the fabrication of memory, is precisely what is uttered, what is shown. Invisible cities, some call it, gateless gates: the labyrinth in the desert, closed window shutters in black and white, in the rain, the all-too-real smells of decomposing waste and grilled meat. Or perfume on one block, pizza and car exhaust on the other. It is very far and very difficult to go there, even for me (especially for me?), even with all these library books around me (especially with all these library books around me?). The temperature is cool, but the titles are confounded as the tongues after the destruction of the tower. Nevertheless I will stay here, at any time willing to acknowledge a *re-mez*, a hint or sign in your mouth or mine, waiting. Ready for the game of strings and threads hanging from a low ceiling in your flat in San Francisco, before we moved in together. Or the room with moisture stains on the walls overlooking an inner patio in Buenos Aires, in winter, empty now.

I want to sit in that cloister again, in the Mission where you took me after I first met your family and saw your childhood house, with the beautiful gardens before me and the adobe walls around me. I want to feel the fresh-though-still air of the inner shade. I want to remember the names of all those bright flowers and oddly shaped cacti, sense the 18th-century construction, see the nests tucked under the archways, hear again the songs of my fellow swallows, the ones you brought me to see knowing I would immediately adopt them, or them me.

Arachne's Red

The oblong gourd holding the bitter herbs of the tea-like drink passes from hand to hand and always back to my grandmother, who, from her seat closest to the stove in the small kitchen, refills it with the nearly boiling water. I follow the gourd circling around the table, an object in space in a confusing orbit around an imagined center, somewhere on the table, where a plateful of pastries (*facturas*) rests. But as the *mate* continues to circle past, my focus shifts and soon I see only the strangely-colored spots on the hands of my grandparents and my mother's aunts: yellow-brown liver spots on their pale wrinkled skin. A nausea fills me as they begin to expand; each time the *mate* completes another orbit around the table, each adult seems to have more of these hideous spots on and around their hands. A nausea that becomes worst as the hot bitter *mate* burns my throat and the caffeine makes my head feel light and the room spins around me.

I lose track of the conversation. At first, they questioned me about my new life in the United States, whether I have new friends, how I like it up there. It is our first visit back to Argentina since leaving and they welcome their grandson/grandnephew into their *mate* circle as if I had never left. But after my brief answers, they go back to their usual topics of conversation, which is okay, since that's how it was when I use to live here. Soon, they are engrossed in discussing the recent developments on the two and three o'clock soap operas, the price of meat and milk and how my cousin Josesito is doing in veterinary school (in his twelfth year of a three-year program).

My Bube Cata hands me the gourd again, another *mate*. I thought I just had one. I hear the words of the old aunts above me, as if it were noise, as if I were sinking. A

feeling of being submerged, of suffocation. I cannot understand what they are saying. Have they broken into Yiddish?
Laughter, loud laughter, that I am sure is directed at me. I
even forget for a moment how to break out of the circle; then,
luckily, I remember just in time: all one has to do is say *gracias*
when handing the *mate* back. After I mutter *gracias,* my Bube
says, *¿Ya está? Sí, sí,* I answer. *Salgo al balcón por un minuto,
¿bueno?* I say and head out to my grandparents' balcony, leaving the oppressing laughter of the spinning kitchen behind
me.

I step outside and, upon closing the glass door, I find
myself surrounded by caged canaries, chirping wildly on their
perches and swings. *¿Tenés muchos amiguitos en Norte América?* they asked. The birds are my grandfather's latest ho-
bby. Do you miss your friends here in Buenos Aires? The
balcony is packed with cages, the bottoms lined with Yiddish
newspapers, each one containing several small yellow birds,
bowls with chopped apples, seeds and cups of water.
Compared to the canaries' loud noises, the traffic from the
city below sounds almost tranquil, like the sound of waves
breaking on a distant shore, trying to reach me even here.
¿Tenés muchos amiguitos en Norte América? My aunts' voices
and harsh laughter resonates in the back of my mind, mixed
with the screaming birds and the fading waves.

That night, after going to sleep, I see my grandmother
peel the oblong liver spots off the back of her fingers and
hands and give them to my grandfather. My Zeide Pedro
collects one from the back of his neck, below his gray hairline,
and others from his wrists and hands, and goes out to the
balcony, where, systematically opening each cage, he feeds
them to the canaries from the palm of his hand. *¿Extrañás a
tus amiguitos argentinos?* They peck at the yellow-brown
oblong delicacies without touching my grandfather's cupped
claw-like hand. They feed from the same hands that undertake

such careful work during the day, measuring, sewing and mending each item of clothing as if it must last a lifetime. After eating the liver spots, the birds become wild and excited, fluttering in their cages, flying desperately in their confinement, bouncing off the walls, as my Zeide closes each one and moves on to the next, thus cleansing himself and my Bube of those spots which, during the day, so openly revealed the passing of time—of long periods of time.

I remember collecting rubber tree leafs in a box under a bed in Buenos Aires. They are everywhere, it is Autumn and they cover the entire courtyard of the school. Nobody has said anything about cutting the tree down yet, but I gather as many as possible, as if I knew this might be the tree's last Fall. What does it take to be happy, we ask now. If only I could lay my hands on that trunk again, feel the rough bark of that tree deeply rooted in the center of Sarmiento Elementary School in my neighborhood of Belgrano. Stand in the cool patio, gather more leafs to place between the pages of my book.

Of course language is an issue now, walking through streets drawn by words. The color of the guitarist in the painting, the flowers that did not survive the winter here, the thing you have been looking for in the junk drawer and cannot seem to find, the tastes of a dinner I can never quite describe. You know how it goes, it's entrails and inner organs as well as ribs and prime cuts, heart, lungs, kidneys, tripe, pancreas, brains, stomach, intestines, udder, balls. Sweetbreads and blood sausages, chuck and short loin, brisket, fore shank, loin end, flank, round, hind shank, rump. And pork sausage sandwiches to start it all off. And the self-serve salad bar and the *panqueque con dulce de leche*, you add, completing the menu for me.

I can see the plaza where I played soccer after school in Buenos Aires, the statue of Alberdi sitting in the center, the playground with sand and swings for the smaller children, the area where we used our school bags to set up goals (*...con mis amiguitos*). The dogs coming into the game, going for the ball, interrupting my precious practice for my future career in Southern California. Now you are going back to your afternoon soccer games, you say, to a defining style of play

on an improvised field in a plaza after school, as if nothing
had changed, as if practice could make perfect, even in
flashbacks. The leafs from the rubber plant tree in the school
courtyard, the barking dogs. After all, we can talk about the
future, but the only thing we ever really have is the past. A
past that we are always seeking to reconstruct.

I was in the fifth grade and did not speak a word of English, Fall 1977. We had just moved to a place called Champaign-Urbana, a small town with two names (both equivocal: it was neither countryside French nor urban) where my father had a research position at the university. There were warnings on television, which my mother translated for us, about kids getting lost in cornfields. One or two disappeared into them every year. You could see the fields from our small apartment: the rows went on forever, the tall stalks in perfect parallel lines extending over the flat terrain to the very horizon, swaying quietly in the wind, as if they were waiting for the stray children. The only subject I understood in school that year was math. The teacher caught me drawing stick figures (some with breasts) in my notebook. She leaned over my desk and yelled. The strange noises she made in English sounded funny to me, it was still blah blah blah with potatoes in your mouth, so I laughed. Under one of the breasted-figures I had written her name: Mrs. Howard. A woman with a man's name, a stick figure with breasts, it made perfect sense. Before moving there, I had never heard of Illinois, had never seen a cornfield, had never met kids who did not play soccer. I had never guessed that our dog, which we had brought with us from Buenos Aires to New York and then to Illinois, would be able to hold her bowels for nearly a week just to avoid going outside to relieve herself during storms that dropped to 60° F below freezing with the wind chill factor.

* * *

Once a day, towards the end of the school year, our whole class was escorted to a special room to practice the national anthem. Mrs. Howard led the class from the piano bench where she sat in front, her head turned to where we—her fifth grade choir—stood on a set of bleachers facing her, singing along. This must have gone on for several weeks, or a couple of months, I don't remember exactly. I could understand a fair amount of English near the end of the fifth grade, but I still did not speak very much. When the class sang loudly I opened my mouth and tried with all my might to join them. Finally, on the day that we were to have learned it, Mrs. Howard just played the piano and left the singing entirely to her students. Most of the class sang along, carrying the tune surprisingly well. Mrs. Howard, short heavy fingers pounding the keys, held her gaze upon us, looking at everyone standing on the three rows of bleachers. She knew the tune by heart, she did not need the John Phillip Sousa score resting on the stand above the keys, and could devote her whole attention to examining her students' output. When the anthem was finished, she got up from her bench and, pointing with pink bloated fingers, excused everyone who had sung. The kids to whom she had pointed got down from the bleachers and went to the other side of the room, leaving a handful of us behind.

Mrs. Howard started the anthem again on the piano, repeating the process several times. I soon realized that the other children who had not sung were shy or frightened, but when there was no one else singing, they eventually released their squeaky voices to the piano's accompaniment of the stars and strips forever. Again and again Mrs. Howard signaled out those who had successfully made their way through the entire anthem. Finally, there were just two of us standing on the bleachers: a squeamish boy to my right and myself. I looked at him briefly: he was staring straight ahead, his round face pale and slightly shaking. I cannot recall his name. Mrs. Howard struck the keys, her accompaniment became incredibly loud, and we both began, *Oh, say can you see...*

The boy continued, poorly, way out of tune, his voice cracking and quivering at points. I tried, but could only hum along. The boy next to me sang all the way to the end—... *and the home of the brave*—then hurried to join the rest of the class by the far wall near the door, leaving me alone on the aluminum bleachers. Mrs. Howard looked at me, her face tight, her hair pulled back into a bun, and let her hands fall hard on the keys once again, filling the room with ghastly chords. I stood there completely mute as she played the entire piano accompaniment to the national anthem. The music was deafening; it weighed heavily upon me; I could not move and, needless to say, could not sing words that I did not know.

* * *

One day after school, despite the warnings on television and those posted around our apartment complex, I wandered into the cornfields. I did not have far to go: they started less then a block from the entrance to our building. To keep my bearings about me, I walked straight into the vast green and yellowish field, following one of the parallel rows that led away from the buildings behind me. After about fifteen or twenty minutes, I stopped and looked around. The rows of corn spread out ahead of me and to the left and right as far as I could see. They reminded me of the geometrical shapes about which I had learned in school in Argentina before we left. Although I had not walked very far, it was already impossible to tell that there was any way out, behind me or otherwise. The straight lines of corn was all there was. The field could have been a couple of acres in size, or it could have extended for hundreds of kilometers. There was no way to know: the shear size of the agricultured maze was dumbfounding. Once in it, as I was, everything outside disappeared and it was just you and the plants of corn and the dark brown clumps of earth at your feet and the hot sun above.

For a moment, I imagined that each plant was a soldier, standing rigidly at attention, and that I was a king examining my many troops. I saluted some plants, gave orders to others and spread words of encouragement throughout since we would be marching off soon. When I got tired of this game, the plants once again became points along parallel lines on an Euclidean plane onto which I had been magically transposed. Then they went back to being just plants of corn and I realized that I had never really examined one of them up close. Thinking of myself as a world famous botanist, I chose a plant to investigate. The ears extended out at various points from the central stalk, smallish corns in groups of two or three wrapped in protective sheaths. They looked funny to me, these half-grown ears bunched together like bananas. Some of them were at eye level, others a bit higher and up, nearly a meter above me, the tassels swayed at the top of the plant, soft and golden. I grabbed the plant I had been examining and pulled it towards me, bending it down to take a closer look at the tassels. By doing this, I inadvertently released their pollen into the air around me. A dense cloud of yellow rained down on my head and shoulders and I was momentarily blinded. Sneezing, my eyes watering out of control, I stumbled away from the plant that I had bothered, my legs working of their own volition to get away as quickly as possible. By the time I stopped, I realized that I had forgotten to pay attention to the direction in which I was going and that I no longer knew which way led back to our apartment. As if that were not enough, by stumbling through the rows, the sharp lancelet-shaped leaves of the plants had produced a number of cuts on my thin arms and legs (it was hot and humid out and I was wearing shorts).

I sat on the dark earth and tried to gather myself. The cuts were like paper cuts: not very deep, but they stung and were very painful. While running away from the plant I had disturbed, I had run into a number of others, so there was still a lot of pollen in the air. The yellowish pockets drifted like buzzing gnats and the clouds of pollen surrounded me, hovering all around. From where I sat, all I could see, regardless of where I looked, were endless stalks of corn. I grabbed a couple of clods of the dark soil, clumped together from generation upon generation of being farmed into elevated rows, and sat with my fists closed tightly and filled with dirt, surrounded by the infinite number of plants, arranged in their geometric perfection, as if they were bars stuck securely into the ground, making escape impossible. At that point, I felt completely swallowed up; I had been absorbed into the huge man-made landscape and completely ignored by it. My presence there was of no significance whatsoever.

What brought me back was something I heard. It was late in the afternoon by now and the wind had picked up. The stalks of corn began to move in slight waves, creating a whistling sound that seemed to start a long distance away from where I sat and lead not to me, but somewhere else, equally far away. The wind rushed quickly through the lines of stalks, raising as it went suggestions of voices, child-like voices. At first it revealed that the voices were trapped, stuck since time had forgotten them in that flat agricultural domain. But then it began to free them and they spoke of a different time and a different landscape, going back to the last major Ice Age that covered North America with clear blue glaciers some 30,000 years ago.

I held the captured soil in my small fists and stood up. The sun was beginning to descend and I remembered that the window from our bathroom faced west and that every night you could see the sun go down over the cornfields from there. With the unknown voices whispering around me, I faced away from the sun and walked straight along one of the rows, careful not to rub anymore against any of the plants. Eventually I saw an opening at the end of the row ahead of me. I came out a few minutes later, only fifty meters or so away from where I had entered. I threw one of the clumps of dirt that I still had in my fist back into the field. The other one I kept, taking minuscule bites of the sweet dark earth as I wandered past the playground, where kids played games that I did not know, driven by words I did not understand. I headed up to our apartment to get cleaned up before my mother returned from work.

From the beginning her words imply music and mathematics, dreams of ships and airplanes. A desire for perfect geometry, my father's physics and my grandfather fixing silver pocket watches in a small corner shop in Buenos Aires. But it is my daughter I am talking about now. Whereas my grandfather dreamt dice that never came up even, I dream blue horses duplicated in mirrors and side windows. My daughter reveals herself to me in parts: rivergreen under long eyelashes here, a hug there. So far away that she looks deceptively static—not yet real. Not yet. I see cylinders of sleeves, half-circles of home-sewn buttons, an approximation of a future. It is foolish to imagine a closed circle (the evasive promise of patrimony), but I cannot help trying. You are not afraid to let me run along these lines, for you know the crucial role you play now, and then. And you know that so much of this is for you, in any case, your smile says as much. You run your fingers through my hair and for a moment I wonder if the circle that needs closing might not be the one you and I have drawn, tonight like other nights, naked on our bed, listening to Duke Ellington and repeating stories of the past, lineages and genealogies.

I was once contained in a transparent picture: the sketch of a violin hidden behind overlapping planes.

You doze off; I am left with my thoughts: a daughter, a future. Broken memories held together by some internal logic, passed on like a baton that refuses to be dropped. My eyes slide over the facts: colonial arches and postmodern angles that constitute the distance between continents and eras. A watchmaker, a physicist, a musician. Why is it that I always disappear in the transformations? Am I truly a translator at heart: less and less visible the better I perform my task? Until the translation finally succeeds—as if one could, without prior knowledge, distinguish between the original and the reflection, as if the mirror did not distort—and past and future become sealed in a decipherable center where I exist and disappear. The strange familiarity of what is found there: the unmistakable moans of a small accordion; an old man buried under a lifetime of discarded fabric; a broken watch; the torn cover of what I once mistook to be an ancient prayer book; your sweet solid voice reciting Neruda to me in English.

Blue horses galloped across our walls at night: we saw ourselves in them and still the walls yielded not.

Everything about her is American, Californian even: the intonation, the clothes, the work ethic, the exercising four days a week, the references to TV shows that I have never heard off. But at the World Cup game she too waves a small Argentine flag, shouts when Battistuta scores a goal, hugs me as we jump in unison with the thousands in the stands. She does not know why—just as I never knew why I had exactly the same feelings when I went with my father to similar games many years ago—but in the unlikely place of a world-class stadium, in the middle of the delirium of the blue and white Argentine celebration, with me at her side, she is at home—just as I felt perfectly at home when I used to see the *selección argentina* as a child with my father—like never before.

And there she is, it is that simple. Waving a miniature Argentine flag at a World Cup game. I see her, and you, beside me.

How we admired the web, lying on a futon raft on the hardwood floors, eyes open in the dark. Even though we never caught sight of Arachne, never knew who wove the intricate patterns in your room. I still remember the 6-foot ceiling, how glad I was to be 5'11". From the upper corner it spread across the entire inner space: bookshelves, mirror, typewriter, from the piles of laundry to the stacks of papers. We just found it there, looked up after sex and saw it over everything. So close to sleep. Like running in a dream, that familiar sensation, a forgotten tongue, the slow motion dash towards an open door. Or searching repeatedly in an over-crowded junk drawer for an item whose name—or purpose, or your urgent need for it—you cannot remember, and yet knowing you must keep looking until you find it. A minute earlier we were lovers, now we were brother and sister and there was no way out. We were caught in a *red*—but that's a slip, you said, you don't mean the color, do you? Playing at cartography in my room again, you asked. No, it was not red, color was not an issue that evening: everything was gray, even the glowing tangles of yarn stacked in the closet. But calling it *red* named the web and its difference, then and there. The tapestry weavers and Minerva's punishment. Silky yet strong as fiberglass, someone had to keep talking and, thankfully, you quickly did. Body tucked under down comforter, face framed by your blond hair on the pillow, you asked if it was a blessing or a curse to hang yourself from the ceiling and weave forever. Then you joked about the buffalo in the park, the bison buddies at the foot of the Rockies that we'd seen that afternoon. And did you know, you continued, that my grandmother's sewing machine (Elaine, the Italian-American grandmother) was the same model Singer as your grandparents'? Oh, and the

Eucalyptus grove beside the house where I grew up outside San Luis Obispo! It too was covered by this web, I remember it now, you said. Spread from branch to branch and between the leafs above, I saw it when I walked through the grove on my way home from school every afternoon, as recognizable as the endless fragrance itself. They're Australian immigrants, you added, they brought the Eucalyptus to California soon after the gold rush, they had felled so many in the mining and for the railroads that they needed imports to replace them. So they brought the Eucalyptus trees, which quickly adapted throughout the state, something about similar climates and rain patterns akin to native lands.

Life is a quilt, you say now.

I was coming to understand your code words, the horse in your backyard that all of you rode at once, the soliloquy in high school, the drive from one Franciscan mission to another, the swallows drawn just for me (or so I liked to believe). I wanted to ask if it was good to see it again, to feel it against your skin, as pervasive now as it was invisible a moment before. But I did not ask. In the bathroom, I looked in the mirror, but the face that I saw there was not my own. And yet the image was familiar: a man's unshaven face, sallow cheeks, thick eyebrows and bulging eyes staring through barb-wired fence. Familiar (like the face of one's father is always familiar in one's dream) as if he'd been waiting there for years, waiting to be seen, waiting for me to see him and say Kaddish—or some other goodbye in a remembered *voseo*. (In the dream I am a little boy and when I am awoken, I ask, "What's a *toque*, papá?" But no one answers.)

I pulled myself away and got into the shower (a desire to become untangled, a desire to resolve the distance between *red* and net), felt the stream of water on my body, heard it hitting the tub around me. When I returned to the room, ducking automatically even though there was an inch to spare, you had fallen asleep. It was time to let the web return to silk (the mulberry bushes painted on the lampshade) and join you under the comforter at last.

I saw him just once, at my Bube Ana's, during a visit the year we lived in Champaign/Urbana. My paternal grandmother had moved to New York in the Fall of 1976, shortly after us, and stayed there when we moved west. My parents sent my sister and I to stay in her crowded hot apartment in Queens for a week in the middle of the Summer, 1977. I remember looking out the window at the other red-bricked buildings quivering in the heat (the kind of heat that can be seen in the air, as if the city was exhaling it) across the cement park and seeing him down below. He walked very quickly, slouched over, both arms around a large brown paper sack filled with bagels and other bread products. He brought these items to my grandmother every day that they were together from the bakery where he worked around the corner from her apartment. His balding head was protected by a frayed gray and black plaid beret and he wore a heavy plain brown jacket even in the heat. It was difficult to tell what the group of black kids playing in the street—they were about my age, ten or eleven years old, five or six of them, lanky and flexible-looking from the window in their tank tops and cut-off jeans—were laughing at as he went by, with his arms around his baked goods, staring down and straight ahead at the sidewalk, his short plump legs covering ground at a rapid pace. It was impossible to tell what the kids were laughing at, or what game they were playing, as my grandmother lived on the twelve floor and all I could hear was high-pitched crackles and sounds that I could not make out, but I knew they were laughing at him, the step-grandfather whom I had just met the night before.

When he walked in, he said a few words in Yiddish and English, neither of which I understood. I still did not speak much English at that time and his strange raspy accent did not help any. Bube Ana yelled to him in Yiddish, a greeting of some sort. He kissed my sister and I on the cheek, his breath strong and bitter, and stripped down to his undershirt for dinner. They ate herring in cream sauce with horse radish on dark rye, while my sister and I had plain bagels, the four of us sitting around a small table in the cramped kitchen. I tried to avoid staring at his hairy arms and back. After dinner, they screamed at each other some more in Yiddish (I remember my sister and I looking at each other as this was going on, expecting one of them to say *kush mich in toches*, but Ana's and Irving's shouting did not include this phrase, so hilarious to my sister and I when we heard our parents use it), while my Bube washed dishes and Irving carefully put the rye and pumpernickel breads back in their plastic bags and then inside brown paper bags. My sister and I played quietly on the yellow-brown carpet in the living room, not knowing if they were really angry at each other or not. At night, I could not sleep: the humidity was so thick that the sheets clung to my body as I lay on the pullout sofa-bed in the living room. The old fan hoisted on a windowsill above the sofa whipped around noisily, and uselessly, in the dark apartment.

As always, there are shreds, impulses in tatters, blocks and spheres, all looking for a form, for their place—and immediately rhythm comes into play. Listening to you from the other side of the table opens a swing, a see-sawing balance that brings me to the surface, conjugates confusion, allows us to endure, like a series of pictures in a slide show, a flashing clarity between us: the phrase, the sentence, always the sentence, and then the paragraph, the page, the section. A book.

You know how difficult it is for me to organize all this, even when you assist in the task. You know that it's not as straightforward as lining up from shortest to tallest in the courtyard of Sarmiento elementary school. Is there, in any case, a particular order that would dictate causality? I refuse to build a scaffolding where none exists. Prospero's tricks must be unveiled, that is how the play ends. But things are different now, as you like to point out: the medications, the changes in our bodies, the loans, the weight of the suitcases, the month-to-month lease agreements. It is alright to bring up lives unlived, places left behind, infinitives or gerunds, there is always time to pack, to find new music teachers. It is alright. Your assurances are as warm clothing in the snow to me. (*For as the dead exist only in us…*) Does it make sense to argue about hand gestures, a kiss on the cheek? Yes and no, you say, speak and language will follow, kiss me on the cheek and habits will form, set the order and a structure will emerge. Or a flow: direction as multifaceted as meaning. I know I must return to Argentina, I know I must be an almost-foreigner in my own Buenos Aires, but the structure can only come from inside—or is it outside?—for where does memory reside? (*And what is a memory that we do not recall?*) The shade from the trees on the sidewalks near Barrancas de

Belgrano will guide you home every time, you say, as in the dream, as in the empty house with the great-aunts in the inner patio, remember?

When you speak I see the chaparral green of San Luis Obispo, rows of books and a spider hanging from a six-foot ceiling, a postcard of an orange VW parked on a side street of an indeterminate city and a girl on a wooden pew (poems as maps, maps as poems), but when you part the curtain there is something new: (*single, distinct, the wave falling*).

And now, within the madwoman's soliloquy: I will dance for you. Just ask the ghosts who kept it alive while you explored places with names like Nueva York, Champaign/ Urbana, San Diego, Providence, Boulder. Or whatever the order is supposed to be, you add, knowing how much good it does me to hear these words in your mouth, like the swallows you showed me in the adobe Mission fluttering to and fro between arches and corner nests. Knowing that the order is not what matters, that stories travel easier than people, that naming cities and relatives and trajectories may just be enough for now. It may just have to be. Knowing that there is something missing, amiss, here and now, between us, as we touch the table at the same time, our fingers outstretched on the varnished pine, the coffee set pushed aside for the time being; that life west of those mountains we see every day from our small kitchen will be unlike and yet no different than it is here in our condominium near the cows; that it is enough for you and me to know that something is missing, that it is not necessary to try to fix it or fill it or whatever one does when one realizes that lack is a central part of everyday life; knowing that for now naming it is enough. Even if we can't agree on what to call it, you ask, smiling again, or in what language to speak of it? Remember, you say, leaving is something we do everyday, so why not make it plural? (*How to compose from these fragments a perfect whole or read in the littered pieces the clear words of truth?*) After all, you go on, Prospero's final trick, his last and greatest deed, is to give away his secrets, to stand naked on the stage, the entire apparatus of his machinery unveiled around and behind him. To stand revealed—which is to say, alone.

MY ZEIDE IN THE POOL

My grandfather has two large cabinets and a full bar that he built himself in the living room of their Florida condominium. The wood is dark mahogany, with smooth rounded edges and fine grain like waves on a beach. The cabinet shelves hold my grandparents' collection of souvenirs from their travels. I spend every available moment, whenever I visit my grandparents, contemplating these beautiful objects, remembrances that do not belong to me, but feel as if they should. There is the Spanish toreador in his elegant golden outfit holding a blood-red cape in front of a bull with colorful ribbons on its ivory horns; a Dutch girl with pointed wooden shoes; two immovable guards from Buckingham Palace; a full carriage, led by two strong and noble horses, inside of which, if you look through one of the side windows, you can see two French ladies in dainty white dresses with a picnic basket between them; a smaller funny little figurine of Napoleon with his bright blue uniform and gold buttons; a Turk with a fuzzy turban; and several tigers and lions that my grandparents claim come from Egypt. There are also several replicas from Argentina that I do recognize: a gaucho swinging his *boleadoras* to lasso a steer, another gaucho sitting on a rock and drinking *mate*, and several regular-sized *mate* gourds, engraved with silver, and the accompanying *bombillas*. The set is always arranged in the same way (now in Florida, before in Buenos Aires), mounted on the wall with long rectangular strips of mirror behind it, multiplying the number of pieces, and three bare bulbs illuminating the collection from above, so as I study it all I see the miniatures on the mahogany, then a shift and the miniatures again reflected back towards me, and finally a partial view of myself, looking on at the many souvenirs, between the shelves and the arrangements from my grandparents' travels.

* * *

Everyone in the family has a theory, but no one really knows why my maternal grandparents moved to Florida, to a retirement complex between Miami and Ft. Lauderdale, after having worked and saved in New York for years to be able to move back to Buenos Aires. Although it has none of the silver or glitz of the California version, their Hollywood, as I saw it when I visited them from Providence shortly after their arrival there, does share with the other the anonymity of movie sets, a sense that a battle is being fought against nature and history as man attempts to create instantaneous communities where there was nothing before but dry chaparral out west, or humid swamplands in the southeast. And then the projection of reality, a simulacrum of life in which people place themselves and write a desired ending.

(*The state with the prettiest name, / the state that floats in brackish water, / held together by mangrove roots / that bear while living oysters in clusters, /*)

The only person that they knew in Hollywood, Florida was their friend Sarah from the Bronx. They had not seen her in fifteen years, but she always said she loved it there, the sun, the tranquility, so we've decided to move there, is what they said before transplanting themselves yet again. Their reasoning was much the same as it had been thirty years before, when they first moved to the U.S. from Argentina: that Buenos Aires was too expensive, that they could not get enough work there, that it was time for them to start anew. *A bi gezunt*, as my Bube likes to say. They never said the word retirement, retirement is not in their vocabulary, even though

Pedro is eighty-seven and Cata seventy-six. They just told us that it was cheaper, that the complex offered great services for seniors, that they would be able to work as much as they wanted to, and then they moved. We're starting over, they said, we're going there to improve our situation, they told us on the telephone, with no room for questions. The next thing we knew they had bought a condominium and moved to Hollywood.

(... *and when dead strew white swamps with skeletons, / dotted as if bombarded, with green hummocks / like ancient cannon-balls sprouting grass.*)

My Bube wrapped the Spanish toreador, the two Buckingham guards, and the Dutch girl with the pointed wooden shoes—along with the collection of *mates* and *bombillas* and the Toledo ashtray with the gold-laced Star of David—individually in tissue paper, then in newspaper, then layered them in a large trunk where they spent several weeks before arriving in their new living room, where she unwrapped each carefully one by one, arranging them in the same location where they were before on the same mahogany cabinet shelves on which I have always admired them, in front of the rectangular mirrors.

My father maintains that my grandmother took my Zeide to Florida so that he would die there alone. He believes she wants him to die out of the way, far from anyone in the family, so no one will see him continue to deteriorate mentally and physically until he enters the inevitable final stages of old age. As if sickness and death were something to hide from, my father says, some kind of unspeakable secret. A *gay ga zinta hate*, one might say. To keep a gross indecent act private, as if Florida were the out-house to which one goes to deposit the excrement and the other bodily wastes of old age and death. She doesn't want anyone to see him die, my father says, it's how they deal with shame.

A small but proud Napoleon, a full French carriage, a Turk with turban and scimitar and a row of Egyptian tigers in front of a mounted set of silver spoons from Sheffield.

But I disagree. Although the process of dying, the breaking down of the human body and its functions, may very well be something that we would rather not think about, something that we might want to keep away from us—far away from us, at least physically if not emotionally; although old age is messy and empty, the reality of it, the failures of the body and the diminishing capacities of the mind devoid of meaning and us unable to stop it; although there is nothing noble about it; although its physical details are exactly the kind of abject material that we try to push deep underground, to have taken care of behind closed doors by someone else, in someone else's house, or better yet, in another town, out-of-state; and although the popularity of retirement complexes is a sure indication of wealth and modernity (because we are modern, because we can afford to do as much, send dying off somewhere where we do not have to think or worry about it—at least where we do not have to see or smell it—where it becomes somebody else's everyday work and preoccupation)—although all of this may be true, I do not believe that this is why my grandmother moved herself and my grandfather to Florida.

No. I believe—as they believe—that they went there exactly for the reasons they claim, in search of something better, looking for a place to work and start over again. It is no secret that my grandfather is dying. My grandmother takes care of him—a nurse in love with her patient fallen into the Atlantic within sight of Ellis Island, a Jewish tailor from Lublin who will never learn English, a mother tending to her ill child, so heavy she can barely lift him anymore. Everyone knows the illness is terminal, only, it could go on for a long time as it is now, needing help with everything, walking, getting to the bathroom, even dressing and eating sometimes. The illness is old age and it has left his life completely empty, he has nothing left, he cannot do any of the things that have always made him who he is: he cannot walk for over an hour before breakfast through city streets as he once did nearly every morning of his life, he cannot work on his Singer, he cannot study the Yiddish newspaper (*Di Presse* in Buenos Aires, *Yiddishes Tageblat* in New York) that he kept in the kitchen and used to line the cages of the birds he once kept hanging in the apartment balcony. All he has is his repetitive exercises in the pool and the Univisión channel turned all the way up in their living room and his nurse, won at the roulette table at the Casino in Mar del Plata on a summer evening the year he quit the Argentine Socialist Party. *Gelt* won from the *goyim gunnif*, he says after the afternoon glass of whiskey.

(*The state full of long S-shaped birds, blue and white, / and unseen hysterical birds who rush up the scale / every time in a tantrum ...*)

But my grandmother is a different story. Something totally unexpected has happened to her: she has undergone a complete and thorough rejuvenation since their arrival in Hollywood, although her found fountain is certainly other than what Ponce de León, or anyone after him, ever imagined. For the first time in her life she applied for and received a driver's license and has bought herself a large American car to sail down the avenues (though thankfully not the highways) of her new state. This alone has revolutionized her life. Although my Zeide can barely get in and out of the large navy blue Chevrolet by himself, although my Zeide sinks deep into the front seat of the car and needs help both putting on and removing his seat belt, this move has allowed my Bube to go far and beyond the one shopping mall where the shuttle from the complex takes its senior residents early in the morning and picks them up right after lunch. She is also working, as they had said they would (even if it is only her now), taking in alterations and repairs. This supplements their Social Security checks with a healthy under-the-table business which has elevated their standard of living considerably (new TV, cable, vacation to Israel and Egypt, trip to Poland, the Chevrolet). Furthermore, her ease with Spanish, Yiddish and, to a large extent, English, mixed with her fluid sociability, has quickly made her one of the most popular residents in the complex, the active *modiste* who fixes and designs at affordable prices and takes good care of her visitors, lending her skillful hands with as much efficacy to the clothes she sews and seamstresses as to the *mate* and *facturas*, which she has found at a Cuban market and which she serves to everyone who enters their condominium.

(*Enormous turtles, helpless and mild, / die and leave their barnacled shells on the beaches, / and their large white skulls with round eye-sockets / twice the size of a man's...*)

In addition, she takes my grandfather with her to all the functions in the complex, including Tuesday dinners at 5 PM, Thursday night bingo—their penchant for gambling now practiced in a game with smaller stakes and better odds—and Saturday evening shows. And she has mapped for herself a complete exercise routine, going to aerobics for seniors four times a week and doing twenty-five sit-ups when she gets up in the morning and before she goes to bed at night. Her thriving mental state and social life, combined with her new healthy physique, plus a nice Florida suntan—as opposed to her usual ghostly Eastern European complexion—has her looking at least ten to fifteen years younger than she is.

Biz hundert un tsvantsik seems to have come true. Indeed, we should all live to 120!

My grandfather paces back and forth in the pool in the middle of the retirement complex, just like the doctors tell him to do. Then, when the heat is too much even for him, he sits in their apartment, drawn back in by the AC. He droops into their sofa in front of their new television, watches whatever is on Univisión and, with the voices of the Venezuelan soap operas above the buzz of the AC, dozes in and out of sleep for hours on end. Occasionally he brings up the idea of getting another eye operation, though the last time that they operated on his cataracts it did not improve his eyesight at all. Meanwhile, my grandmother runs around, energized, working, independent even as she takes care of everything he needs, younger and more active than at any other time in her life, even smiling occasionally, knowing the move to Florida was a good idea from the very beginning.

I talk about beginnings but I know that eventually I will have to end all this, decide on an order, draw a map even if the scale is unrecognizable. Go on, you say, let the knots go, close the lined notebooks once and for all. So you think I should go back to Argentina? Is this table between us not enough? What about our move to the Bay Area? And what if I land in Buenos Aires and keep speaking English? What if don Domingo is closed? How can I turn southeast when everything up to here has been north and west? Is it possible, in any case, to journey home, to be lost in exile and found in translation?

My city is memories of a blue guitarist discussed at a window table over a *cortado*, an interrupted tram line that takes me to the stadium, shady walks on cobbled sidewalks leading to the house in the dream, piano staircases going in and out of a cold inner patio, a key in my pocket that does not fit into any lock I try. Everything in the city is familiar, the streets and their names, the restaurants and the cafés, the smells and the sounds, how people walk and greet each other, the rudeness of the drivers, the best route to tell the taxicab driver—the city is the same but I am different, it is my city but I am a foreigner there. Again.

This is how it really begins. When you realize that the problem is not that you have left, you say, but that you are still leaving; when you figure that out, then we can begin, we can leave the compass and the Kabbalah alone, we can be content with looking out the window and not worry whether it's the Andes or the Rockies.

I am here illicitly, passport or no passport. I was born in translation, conceived in Buenos Aires by the children of Polish Jews and delivered in a hospital in the Bronx by a sweaty Indian intern and a Puerto Rican nurse, everyone shouting in different tongues. And now you tell it back to me from the spotted shadows of a Eucalyptus grove. These are not my lines, I am meant to tell the fictions of others, even my birth is not my own.

One's stories are never one's own, you say, whether they be about ghosts or other relatives. Remember: you can only lose what you never really had. I know that this time taken for you and me is precisely that: taken, as in stolen, researched with the conviction that the traces that we do not see or expect, the spidery handwriting on the back of your postcards, form a net as compelling as Penelope's. *Red, nos gusta ese pequeño juego, ¿no?, de la red en inglés al color morado de tus mejillas cuando hacemos el amor.* Red, as in in the red, the theft of translating the many selves that the past presents the future to remake.

The translator must face difference and stand before it, in the abyss of the in-between, as steady as the bricklayers of Babel, as steady as Job. The translator must reside in that difference, in a difference that is exile.

Even when we put several languages into play there is still no name to give it, a sensation in and of the body, the slight touch of fingertips sliding over nearly invisible hairs, locating flesh, pressing, loving, the waves of sound that modulate to tell of life. I am not ready to organize all this, to demand an order where I know only diverging lines, patterns drawn by the moisture on the walls: clouds and horses one day, the grid of a city map the next. But you have no choice, you say; and though I offer my help, you add, we both know that it is not I who must line up the sections—it is you who must imagine time as if it were space. Sitting on the bed in our parents' bedroom was as confining as the circle of the aunts yipping in Yiddish and slurping *mate* in the humidity of the inner patio. At times like that we—you and I, my sister and I, my mother with her family, my father in his father's shop, my grandparents and the Singer, ¡*Merde!*—long for other places, we yearn to travel, to cross oceans and large masses of land, to take ships and trains and airplanes and cars, to see landscapes that we know from books, to eat meals with exotic flavors and feel something in our ear that is not our tongue. But what is left, I wonder, after this has happened so many times only to happen many times again? Just add to it, you say quickly, before I get a chance to protest, speak and listen with your incompleteness, go ahead, add your doubts as if they were integrals in an equation without rules, as your father might say. Go ahead, before you leave again.

In the summer of 1978 we moved from Champaign-Urbana to San Diego in an old white station wagon. We had our Argentine mutt with us (my sister and I wouldn't hear of leaving her behind, especially since we'd already brought her from Buenos Aires to New York to Illinois), so we were forced to make innumerable stops along the way. Knowing that our progress would be slow, my parents decided to visit a few tourist spots on the cross-country move. While hurrying through Iowa and Kansas and the endless fields of corn with which we were more than familiar after nearly a year in Illinois, I wondered if all of America was a land-locked ocean of swaying stalks, food-producing fields into which one or two children disappeared every year. But eventually the landscape changed. After the corn there were mountains and a few cities and plateaus and vast plains and a ghost town and many road-side diners, but of all the places where we stopped, all I remember is taking a photograph with an Indian in front of the capitol in Denver, standing at the exact spot of the four corners and yelling ¡*Merde*! with my sister, walking briefly along the rim of the Grand Canyon and getting out of the air conditioned station wagon to a 95° night in Phoenix, Arizona.

Throughout the two-week trip, I carried an insect jar with me. I poked holes in the lid to help the bugs stay alive. Before we were even out of Illinois, somewhere near Springfield—at our first stop, not far from where I had gone on a field trip with my fifth grade class to see Lincoln's log cabin—I caught a cricket at a rest stop, making sure not to hurt it. At the next stop, I released it into a patch of tall grass. I continued doing this, catching one or more crickets at one rest stop and releasing them at the next. I hid the jar with me in the back seat; it would have been easy to scare my sister, or play some kind of game with her and the bugs, but I didn't want to risk having the jar get taken away from me. Thanks to the confusion in the car with the dog and our bags all jammed in the back, it was not difficult to keep the crickets a secret. I kept catching and releasing them at new locations throughout the trip. I wanted them to see more than their one stretch of lawn where I found them, usually near the bathrooms. I wanted them to see the world.

When you and I started all this, by chance, as all meetings are by chance (how else, how else?), I had but one thing to say— that I am not from here—and I said it (I had to say it) as a form of introduction. Hello, my name is such and such, hazelnut is my favorite kind of cake, you may not hear or recognize my accent at first, but I am not from here. (What does it mean to be from here? What does it mean to be from anywhere, really? If we forget our grandparents we are from nowhere.) You liked that I said it in English, that I insisted that English was not my language and that I did so in English, the perfect immigrant trap, you called it. Now the statement must be amended, as the introductions are long over and we are closer to practicing goodbyes than anything else. Besides, it was easier that way, for you to introduce yourself like that, because it's one thing to say that you're not from here, to imply that you are from somewhere else—Buenos Aires, Lublin, Orsay, Nueva York, who knows?—and another to say (to realize) that you are from nowhere at all. (I am not from here.) Nowhere. Or perhaps that, in your case, being from a place only gains meaning once you have left that place: leaving the burning of the second temple made your family Jewish, leaving Lublin and Warsaw made your family Polish Jews, leaving Buenos Aires made you Argentine Polish Jews, etc, etc. But how useful, we wonder now, is that much-talked-about critical distance? What good is it when you are tired, when you feel like going home, when you want to follow the cobble-stoned shade near Barrancas de Belgrano to your apartment on 3 de Febrero? What good is it when you want an *asado*, or herring in cream sauce with rye bread, or *panqueques con dulce de leche*, or *mate y facturas*, or gefilte fish and *ravioles*, or whatever strange combination one's memory conjures to call home on any particular day?

Figuring out which verb tense to use.

Touring the missions was your idea. It made sense, you had heard enough about my family to introduce me to yours. And the Spanish connection worked, too, despite our skepticism about missionaries of all sorts. I met your family in San Luis Obispo, fell for the phonetic spelling and the stories of the children learning to shear lambs in 4-H, heard about the year your sister spent in a body cast as a little girl and her penchant for eating entire blocks of butter when no one was looking, played Yatzhee with your mother on her kitchen table, remembered my Zeide Ignacio playing *la Generala* in a café in Villa Crespo, remembered the day my Zeide Ignacio's numbers came up (rather: remembered the stories of my Zeide Ignacio playing *la Generala* in a café in Villa Crespo while his son covered the shop for him). The next day I touched the outside of your house, smelled the Eucalyptus grove that you smelled everyday on your way to school as a child (*el interminable olor de eucalyptus...*). Learned that your parents had never heard a mass in Latin and that your mother could speak for hours on end about who'd had a baby, or who was pregnant, or who'd had a serious illness within a twenty-mile radius. After meals I snuck away for long walks, read the names of the neighboring streets, stopped at the creek to wonder if one day my daughter would run down the banks, while her grandparents watched from above, to throw rocks into the moving waters below (*aguas en movimiento anticipando las piedritas que arrojará mi hija desde este mismo sitio...*). On the other side, up a steep hill, I saw the theater designed by Julia Morgan perched against the horizon: San Luis Obispo's miniature castle for flappers always ready to jitter bug—or so I thought as I thought of you.

* * *

Touring the missions provided us with our own west coast map. The one in San Francisco—which, in 1776, was the sixth of the twenty-one California missions founded by the Spanish Franciscans between 1769 and 1823—was an excuse to remember Vertigo and see a part of the city, with the palm trees down the middle of the rolling Dolores, which we identified at once as our future home. We skipped the two north of San Francisco—Solano (1823) and San Rafael Arcángel (1817)—and headed south with a specific destination in mind. We drove down the coast in your VW Thing, rolled along with all the windows down since the exhaust seemed to be redirected into the car instead of out the back. We made brief stops along El Camino Real at Santa Clara de Asis (1777), Santa Cruz (1791) and Nuestra Señora de la Soledad (1791), and spent a few days at your parents' in San Luis Obispo de Tolosa (1772) (the church that your parents, and you on Easter and Christmas, still attend). We left San Luis Obispo and stopped only in Santa Barbara (1786) before reaching our southern-most point, south of Los Angeles and Irvine: San Juan Capistrano (1776).

As we pulled off the I 5 in Orange County I recalled a lesson from elementary school in Buenos Aires, or from some field trip in junior high, or from the Encyclopedia Britannica in San Diego. I could not remember when or where I had learned this, but somehow I knew all about them. About the Scout Swallows that precede the main flock by a few days, as if to clear the way for the main flock of swallows to arrive at the Old Mission of Capistrano. About the fact that their arrival always coincides with St. Joseph's Day (March 19, as we rolled in), when the flittery little birds begin to arrive and immediately set to work rebuilding their mud nests, clinging to the ruins of the old stone church. About how their point of origin (somewhere in the Southern Hemisphere) had been a mystery for such a long time, until an ornithologist in the early twentieth century tracked the swallows back to the small town of Goya (population 8,442), in the province of Corrientes, on the edge of the deep Paraná river, in Argentina—where the birds' point of origin (somewhere in the Northern Hemisphere) had been a mystery for such a long time. About the fact that the swallows leave Goya on February 18th, in successive bands, and that they fly at an altitutde of more than 2,000 kilometers to take advantage of the tail winds and to avoid plundering birds. That they fly fifteen hours—without eating or drinking, so as to make better time—and cover approximately 450 kilometers per day. That the flight that begins in Goya follows the valleys of the Paraná and Paraguay rivers until reaching Lake Mirin, following the dynamic currents that produce the large masses of southern winds that move towards the equator. That after Mirin, their route changes to the west, in search of the valleys of the Andes and later, crossing the equator, they go to a higher flight altitude to take advantage of the currents that produce the large masses of air that move towards the North Pole. That they do not cross the Andes until they have reached the Gulf of Mexico, where, by way of the Yucatan, they look for the west and the Pacific, in order to fly along the shore of Baja California and enter the valley of Riverside and then down to San Juan Capistrano. That the entire trip is about 12,000 kilometers each way.

We toured the modest inside of the church, then went back outside, walked under the arches and sat in the cloister to hear the bells of the old Franciscan monastery ring and watch the first group of swallows—there they are, the scouts, we said as we pointed to the sky—circle around, reconnoitering the terrain, searching for their old nests or for a good spot underneath the eaves to build a new one. We sat for a long time in the shade of the cloister, long after the bells had ceased ringing, long after we had discussed homing mechanisms that make such migrations possible, just watching the fluttering of the swallows as they worked to settle in their northern nests. We finally left when it started to get dark, at which point I remembered another part of the lesson: that the swallows always take flight again on the Day of San Juan (October 23), that one morning they just leave their nests, that they fly up and circle the Mission one last time before rising to higher elevations for their return-trip, as if bidding farewell—at least until the following year—to the Jewel of All Missions, San Juan Capistrano.

*   *   *

And now you tell me that the problem with claiming that I am not from here, that I am not from this or that other particular place, the problem, the way I see it, you say, is that if you don't claim any of these places, how can you claim any of their tongues? The problem and the solution at once, that is, to speak the language of a place and not be of that place, to have that experience with any language one speaks, to not have a native tongue. For if you are not the river, you add with a quick glance from the other side of the table, the cup of coffee touching your lips softly, warmth feeling heat and steam, smiling between cup and brow, framed in blond mischief, if you are not the river you are the desert, and below the scorching sun, irregardless of latitude (of one's relationship with the lines of the tropics) there is only you and the calcined stones which will, with time (soon enough, timepiece or no timepiece to measure with), turn to sand and drift, carried by burning winds, always airborne, never touching ground again, roots to remain a mangled concept learned from books, hearing only rustling and a confused blowing in your ears (the swallows gone too?), a completely unorganized and pattern-free grouping of sounds never to approximate a tongue, only the wheezing and coughing of your father, of your mother, your little sister gone, alone at the end as at the beginning, that is the I without the you. Don't forget the one thing we both said from the beginning, which we repeat even louder now near the end: welcome home.

It is the first day of the sixth grade and Mr. Richards wants to get straight to work. He lines everyone up towards the back in alphabetical order, from a to z, he says, left to right, there you go kids. We leave the safety of the large tables with our backpacks and pens and pencils and notebooks sprawled all over them and take our places as indicated, facing the front of the classroom, standing against the back wall. The board is green, an enormous backdrop framing the bony outline of the new teacher. It is the first day of the school year and everyone is fidgety. We have arrived in San Diego. Some pull their pants up, shift their weight from one leg to the other, tug at their shirt ends; one rubs the back of his hand over his runny nose, snivels loudly, makes others giggle and fidget some more. Who is this new teacher, anyway? What is going on, what kind of activity is this? And on the very first day of classes! Who is this Mr. Richards?

Finally, after a fair amount of shoving and adjusting, everyone more or less settles into place, standing at attention with their backs to the wall. This first task accomplished, the teacher straightens himself and announces the reason for lining us up like this. We are going to have a spelling bee, he says in a loud clear voice which apparently explains everything to the sixth graders. They all understand, they all know why they have been asked to get up from the tables, to line up in alphabetical order like that. They all know what is about to take place, what this first activity of the year is all about. Makes perfect sense, we're gonna have a little spelling bee, their thoughts almost audible. Just a little game to start the year off, you've played this before, Mr. Richards continues, the words surprisingly loud from such a thin-framed man. You're in the sixth grade now, the oldest class in the school. I know you just had a long summer break, but it's time to get your brains thinking again. Just a quick spelling bee to get you into school mode. A real thinking game, so wake up.

So they begin to concentrate, to focus in on where they are, the schoolroom, the new teacher in front of them. This is going to be fun, a spelling bee, I'm gonna do good, I can do this, the students say with their facial expressions. Their eyes, sharper by the moment, are now fixed on the exceedingly thin and tall teacher, pacing in front of the green board like an automated skeleton, far across on the other side of the deserted chairs and tables with all our belongings spread on top of them. Thin and tall, he stops, examines his new students through his spectacles, looks them up and down, left to right, and turns to pace the length of the green board again. Lets himself and his words be measured carefully. We are going to have a spelling bee, a quiz, a game to get everyone involved from the very first day of the school year, a real thinking game.

But not everyone in the class has understood. For there is a skeletal monster, a looming frame, branches thin as a stick figure's moving in and out of bubbling green depths. Sounds that form strange words burst from an opening that must be a mouth, below round glass spheres, dance devilish green patterns, split apart, loose particles in a hot room, rejoin and strike as unforgiving waves. Seasick, seasick, black water climbing up canyon walls, bony fingers reaching, flexing, their drive to grab and pull down, down forever unyielding. The thunderous crash of a thousand such waves on a thousand and one different shores. And behind it all the skeleton beast and the waving flag.

Okay, let's get started, Mr. Richards says, picking up the class list from his organized desk at the front of the class. He begins to call out names and words, names and words I have never heard before. Becky Armstrong, mansion. And the girl on the opposite side of the line answers, mansion. m-a-n-s-i-o-n. Very good, Mr. Richards says. Clashing sounds from deep green depths. Now Brian Lindbergh, telephone. The boy next to the first girl straightens up and says, t-e-l-e-p-h-o-n-e. I understand, I think I understand. Everyone is extremely serious, Mr. Richards stares at the class list held firmly before him, then enunciates a name and a word for each one. Words come from the man's thin lips, the mouth opening quickly underneath the spectacled dark eyes swimming in a slippery substance. His thin arms never move at all, they just grip the list, and he barely shifts his pointed chin and huge thick glasses from the paper to look at the line of students standing at attention against the wall. He speaks names and words slowly and deliberately, mouthing each syllable, firing them across the deserted tables and chairs, the notebooks, pens, pencils and erasers that seem an infinity away from this back wall. The mass behind him moves, fluctuates, comes at me in waves, I see only the teacher and that green and feel dizzy, nauseous. I understand, I think I understand. But how does he know what word to give each kid? The students always respond in turn, spell the words that accompany their names carefully—letters thrown back at the stiff instructor, at a mouth that is a black oval of pasty flesh.

C-l-i-m-b. Climb, the girl to my left has finished spelling climb. No one has made a mistake by the time that my first word finally arrives, at the end of the alphabet as always, standing as ready as I can. Sur-ghio Weiss-men, ghost. I hear both my names mispronounced by the stick figure with the thundering voice in front of the blurry green before me. It is my turn, I know, I have to speak up now, lost under the weight of all that green. Ghost. Ghost? G-o-s-t? I manage to squeak back across the shifting room. The giggles that arise from several of the kids in line tell me at once that I am wrong. I'm sorry, you forgot the H, there is a silent H in ghost, Sirgeo (my name mispronounced again). *¿Una H? ¿Una H muda? ¿Para qué carajo hace falta una H en ghost?* I go back to my seat. The game continues without me.

One of the first things my parents did when we moved into our new house in San Diego was to put up a framed reproduction of *The Old Guitar Player* (*The Blind Guitarist*). They hung it on the wall facing the dining room, between a bookshelf—which, along with several *mates* from Argentina, soon became filled with the thirty volumes of the eleventh edition of the Encyclopedia Britannica and the monthly issues of National Geographic—and the garage door. We always used this door to go in and out of the house instead of the front one. We would walk past the washer and dryer, between the Ford Fairmont station wagon and the Datsun 210 that soon joined it, push open the garage door, go under it and out into the driveway that looked across to other houses much like our own. The driveway where I learned to play catch by myself.

Sallow cheeks, sharp cheekbones, emaciated frame. Face drawn, eyes retreating, looking nowhere and everywhere at once. Pulling me to him. Legs crossed under him, neck of guitar above his shoulder, cradling diagonals.

I see him whenever I look up from the dinner table. My father talks about his new job at a company with many Ss and mainframe computers: Systems, Science & Software: S to the third power: S-Cubed. My mother compares everything with Argentina. Nothing measures up. My sister tells my parents about her new classmates in the second grade, the new games she is learning to play in the schoolyard during recess and lunch. Tether ball and four square. I look up from my plate and see him guarding the exit, his instrument on his lap. Is he there to keep strangers from coming in, or any of us from going out?

Draped in blue. Old, but not in years. Tired, infinitely tired, he does not seem blind to me. Bent over his guitar, long slender fingers on the extended neck, playing notes that drop one by one into an ocean of color.

You and I sit at our kitchen table. It is your favorite poem, you say, and I am amazed to see him again. Here I look up and see you, your lips moving in our small kitchen. Beyond, outside the sliding glass door that leads to the brief plot of land that accompanies our rented condominium, glimpses of snowy peaks point westward. Mountains we will cross before too long. And between you and me the poem that you read, the angles and a weight—of gravity, or history.

Le vieux guitarriste aveugle is his name, 1903, oil on wood. Wrapped in grief, he plays his tune in perfect pitch.

I dream of a house in which I have never lived. Everything is familiar, but changed somehow. I expect people to be there who are not. The walls have memories, like us, like our bodies. They whisper in a language that I do not speak but am able to understand. They know me and want me to know them as well. But it is impossible. It is only a dream and must be left behind.

Every night, at dinner, I would look up and discover another shade of blue, another detail. There were more stories about my father's work. And my mother had begun studying for the C-Best to get her equivalency and be able to teach. Things were going well. We were going to be able to stay. Make San Diego our home. Take swimming lessons. Get a bicycle for New Year's.

The angles too spoke to me, the head leaning over the body. Opening paths by creating wakes, note by note, drop by drop. Textured light from a window behind falling with heavy hues, blue down to his bare feet.

The house in the dream has no colors, no paintings on the walls. Instead, an inner patio dominates a series of connected rooms, a flight of stairs and a melody somewhere down the hall. It is inhabited yet empty, full of voices and echoes, but there is no one to utter them. It has a few mirrors that become doors and others that do not.

You have your own dream, of course, looking for something in a junk drawer. The scent from the Eucalyptus grove drifting in through the open window. In between we have him, for now, the blue guitarist over dinner. Or, better yet, the solitary music he plays to himself every night, not knowing that some, like us, are spying on him. Ignoring anyone who dares say that he is mad—for he is not! He is not!

A sense of life, past and present, bowing us down, changing things, adding weight. Bringing the blue earth closer to us everyday.

No elementary school violin recitals for me. No rides for Ryan (Japanese mother, American father), no rides for Lijlijana (Bosnian mother, American father). No Saturday morning class picnics under the Coronado bridge. No arguing over what music to listen to on the way to preschool. Does it make any sense to say that I will miss these things—no violin recitals!—even if I have never had them? Not to mention the swallows flying in and out of your mouth, so long ago already, and poem maps taut enough to bend continents. No. No more drives west for you and I, I have faced southeast long enough, I must return, I must jump in the water and swim against the tide, any river will do, they all converge at the source anyway, I must swim back, find the *desembocura*, the Tigre delta at the end of the Paraná, I must.

And if the original turns out to be unfaithful to the translation?

Abandoning a future is not unlike leaving the past: in both cases one has the sensation that one need not have left, that one can still go back and relive the other paths, unlived. One believes that choices are not irreversible. In both cases, however, that sensation is completely unfounded. If you are leaving, at least be honest, you say. There is no reversibility option in life—and it is only in this respect that the past and the future are truly the same: neither is reversible. Besides, ghosts do better long distance, they always have, the yellowing page is the clearest example, frayed fabrics and moth-eaten suits, they need all that space—geographic as well as temporal—to be ghosts. Distance is the point of departure, remember, the expression is yours, don't forget it now. Leave here, you say, and I will become your ghost—however you spell it, however you pronounce it—but don't let that comfort you. I have my own lines, as you like to say, but they are lines without ghosts, no echoes off abandoned walls, no shadows in emptied patios, no, my lines—you saw it yourself—are fists of earth and eucalyptus bark, a refurbished VW still running between San Francisco and San Juan Capistrano, a room with a short ceiling and webs in the corners, piles of sweaters, half-finished lists and outdated coupons, the dog that ate apples in an open yard, that and more and no ghosts anywhere to be found, for I can touch my condition, I can touch it, and so can you.

*   *   *

Our disagreements are always the same: we fight over signifiers, locations on a map, our bodies and their positioning, plans for the weekend and a checking account that never balances. We argue over language, in English, and as I translate myself for you I lose myself and gain you, and perhaps, sometimes, when our days have not gone too badly and we have the right music on (Nina Simone perhaps) and the coffee settles us down even as it alerts us to the other, sometimes, sitting at the table across from the other or lying side by side in bed, it flows in the other direction as well, but only sometimes, and still primarily in English.

The house that I am trying to recall is empty, but it is not abandoned, there is a difference there. I insist: the house in my notebooks is empty, but it is not deserted, you've heard the voices yourself. But how can you claim that it is not abandoned, you ask, when your only references to the house are of ghosts and dreams?

In the dream, I never know if I am awake or asleep, I am always trying to wake up to confirm that I am dreaming. In the dream, my father is nearby, even if I cannot see him, and when he talks to me I understand what he is saying, but not the language in which he speaks. In the dream, I see the house from outside, I am never completely inside, and I am afraid to leave.

* * *

No, there are no ghosts in my lineage, you say again, my folks are here for good and so am I, I'll travel all you want but I will always return to California, I don't need to ask any questions to know where I'm from, I open my mouth and I am those swallows that you're so fond of. I am the song and the song is the body, you add. You are the one with spirits, not I, I have postcards from the Jersey coast, scenes of work from Pittsburgh, Akron, Ohio, something from Cabarrus County and a note about adult literacy in Boston, I am both the pictures on the front and the scribblings on the back, you say, there is no differentiation for me, that's your business, all that splitting, images and words, as if life really consisted of criss-crossing conversations. But it's not, not for me, not for you. No utopic affirmation to conclude this interior mono-logue. It's all one vast flat deserted terrain, my love (*mi amor*), the horizon is an illusion, the landscape goes on forever, you are the one who first mentioned the pampas, you say, even though you've lived in an apartment overlooking a busy av-enue for hundreds of years, at least until you got lost in those cornfields in the Midwest. Now I am the landscape and the mountains and the forests and the rivers and the oceans, you say, and you cannot leave me anymore than you can leave the earth, ashes remain in heaps of words, everyone struggles with the wind, or the tide, a planet spinning on its axis, think-ing they will reach the horizon, the imposing line of distance, thinking it will be different for them, different for them this time, but it never is. Enjoy the water, love (*mi querido*), don't fight it, it's not always this wet and slippery in here, you say, you should know that by know, splash inside while you can, you will only miss it when you are dry and hot and alone again, thinking there was a city or a friend at the end of the line, thinking, still in a language not your own, still.

I am back with my Zeide Pedro walking to and fro in the shallow end of the pool in the retirement complex in Hollywood, far from the tailor's shop in the Bronx where I pulled loose pieces of string that clung to my Zeide's pants (as he sewed on the Singer and listened to the radio), or where I gathered the pins from the orange-brown carpet and stuck them into a cushion for my Bube Cata in return for a hard candy from the glass bowl by the front door. A Polish Jew all alone in the Florida heat, convinced that with each length of the pool his legs are getting stronger and that soon he will be able to walk on firm ground at a more or less normal pace, without fear of falling, without needing the cane or my grandmother's arm to help him along. That he will be able to walk, perhaps for half an hour, if not for all those hours that he walked before, in Buenos Aires, in New York, covering every neighborhood on the edge of the Río de la Plata, finding his way around the newly-discovered Bronx, winding through the cities' grids as they came to life—every morning of his life in the north and in the south, in both witness to an organic machine sluggishly awaking each new day.

Prior to this, for eight years in Buenos Aires, in semi-retirement, around the Parque Centenario, weaving his way toward Avenida Rivadavia and across to the southern half of the city; before that, for twelve years in New York, choosing his way through what he considered the safe parts of the Bronx; before that, for half a century in Buenos Aires, covering the entire cosmopolis, from El Once to Palermo, from Retiro to Flores, from Belgrano to San Telmo; in every case, always identifying the places where Yiddish was welcome (a kiosk here, a butcher shop or bakery there). And always these two hours of walking, beginning before dawn at times, followed by reading the newspaper he would have picked up somewhere along the way, over *mate* and *facturas* (which he would have also gotten during his excursion), and a full day of tailoring not yet begun.

But where did he walk before? Where did he walk before he married my grandmother, before he traveled alone from Poland to Argentina? A man who cannot tell his grandchildren the year in which he was born. *¿Por qué no sabe? ¿Por qué no sabe?* I ask my Bube. *Así era antes,* my grandmother shrugs, tilts her head. Then he switches to Yiddish, although he must know that my sister and I do not understand. The conversation ends. I never find out where he walked before, what it was like before Argentina. I never learn if he also walked in Poland, or when, or what he saw or did there. The place, the people—whatever there was before Buenos Aires—is something that I never get to. Instead, Yiddish— the strange articulations framed by the perfectly trimmed white goatee into which my Zeide always switches when this topic comes up—becomes that place, a mysterious world I cannot see, hear, or smell, steps I will never be able to follow.

(*Thirty or more buzzards are drifting down, down, down, / ...*)

Surrounded by the unused plastic lawn furniture, the recreation center and administrative offices of the complex, he trudges back and forth, pushing against the immovable clear-blue water, progressing even slower than he does outside. It is slow motion and it fits him these days: his quiet moods and measured movements. He walks from one side of the pool to the other, touches the edge, raises his hands cupped with water to refresh his face, turns around, heads back for the other side of the shallow end. Above the glare of the water, his head is like a gleaming helmet: the strands of silver hair combed back over the balding spot on his shining head, held in place as if by magic even in the pool, kept there by the pomade that he applies every morning when he awakes—an early morning ritual which, for some reason, I have always enjoyed observing whenever I stay with my grandparents (and which, until recently, indicated that he was about to head out for his walk). Although his hair has always been combed back with pomade like that, however, what really defines his face is his white goatee, glimmering now just above the shifting sky blue water. A swan-white growth of stiff hair, noble though foreign, a crown misplaced, situated on his chin instead of above his handsome gray face. A facial key worn proudly behind which the enigmas of age and migration reside.

Completely alone under the heavy humid air, the lonely struggle against a large body of water, repeated over and over again, with no one to witness the effort (I watch from the shade, off to a side of the pool, where my Zeide seems to have forgotten my presence altogether), going on in the unshakable belief that he is getting better with each length, as if effort alone, if sufficiently heartfelt, could reverse his approaching ninety years of life. Going on because that is what he has always done.

(over something they have spotted in the swamp, / ...)

It is over 90° F with 95% humidity. My Zeide is the only one in the pool. Everyone else in the complex is inside. Outside the water, he can hardly walk. Aided by a cane which he has finally agreed to use on one side, and my grandmother on the other (or me, on this occasion), it takes him twenty-five minutes to get to the pool from their condominium, a block and a half away. (By the time we reach the pool, the only thing I can handle is sitting down in the shade near the outdoor showers.) When he is in that body of water, moving slowly but moving nonetheless, there is only the slight splashing and his breathing and the steady progress and no other sounds at all. There is no one to tell him about the neighbor Mrs. Stein who is so happy with her husband's new wheel chair. No one to tell him to wake up, Pedro, why is he watching television so loud if he's just going to doze off. No one to tell him to use a walker, that octogenarian legs need assistance, that there is no shame in that. No one. Only him and the vast watery silence. Only him, from one side of the pool to the other.

Am I the only one looking? Him alone, I with my eyes glued to him. It haunts me, the image of my Zeide in the pool. I feel his prickly whiskers against my cheek the last time I kissed him goodbye. His absolute aloneness, the same endless pacing back and forth, the hot quiet of the afternoon broken only by the occasional sound of the water splashing around him. Eighty-seven years of life culminating in this limited set of movements repeated every day in this most seemingly arbitrary and isolated place in the world. And the longer he keeps at it, the more absurd it becomes. This going back and forth becoming who he is now, replacing who he used to be. His three-month voyage from Europe to Argentina to avoid being drafted into the Polish Army in 1929. The decades of tailoring with my grandmother in Buenos Aires. His numerous financial ups and downs, his South American summer days on the beach in Mar del Plata and nights dreaming around a spinning roulette wheel in the Casino, four thousand, six hundred and eighty days of work in New York without a vacation. Eighty-seven years, and now this.

(*in circles like stirred-up flakes of sediment / sinking through the water.*)

In every move, with every step, the muscles in his face are set, his impressive white goatee and shining silver hair combed back, his gray eyes staring straight ahead as if his destination were not the other side of the shallow end but some distant place that only he can see. Repetition, a peaceful dream, an exercise in futility. Back and forth in the pool, a show of strength against the forces of nature, personified by the water before and against time itself. To and fro, an old man's unwillingness to give in. The constant movement in the water under the sun, always the same, always alone, a glimpse—as I see my Zeide Pedro now—of a clenched hand reaching toward the calcined edge on the other side of the pool, an unparting sea still left to cross.

LEAVING

It is impossible for me to goodbye to you. No, wait, I'd like to try again. I was going to say something different, I was going to say that to say goodbye to you is to say goodbye to a line we had but only begun to trace, it is to say goodbye to a third I will never know. You will be fine without me, I know, it is vain of me to think otherwise. I must go back to Argentina, you've said it yourself (haven't you?), that is the only reasonable end for all this, we fall asleep on a queen-size bed—the long walk in the humid heat of New England to the mattress outlet before the purchase of the Civic even—and dream of floating in a river of salt water. We cross the river never to come back, metamnesia, you say, remember? And although we cannot recall the dream when we awake we are certain of its accuracy. Some people speak of destiny. But destiny makes no sense at the point of bifurcation, does it, you ask and breathe in and inadvertently the sound is of wind gathering before a storm. And fire would make four. But you exhale silently and your breathing returns to normal, the glitch almost unnoticed: a wave falling only to be followed by other waves: *la hermosura del vacío creado por la memoria del gerundio.*

The joining of the seams, fabric guided by hands steady though marked by liver spots. Mounted clocks frozen on different time zones all waiting for the absent watchmaker. Does the father always leave in your story, you ask. A hundred years or a thousand nights, we will never reach the end of either, we do not want to reach the end of either, we cannot possibly reach the end of either. (*Then Abraham gave up the ghost, and died in a good old age, an old man, and full of years; and was gathered to his people.*) You should not have started with the numbers, now we must allow analytic calculations to reenter the scene, the threes and fours of Kabbalistic detective tales, *las cifras que siempre engañan*— and of course my father again. Give me my ball back, I'm going to the park to play soccer, I'll use my shoes to mark the goals and play barefoot, *carajo*. I thought you traded your soccer ball for a baseball mitt, you say, thinking of yourself now, of which I am glad although I cannot say so. But it does not matter, I am going, no more Franciscan missions for me, I cannot grow geraniums in the snow, tomorrow I buy my ticket and fly south. Will it explode, this borrowed ticket of yours, you ask, is that what you are hoping for? I am in trouble and I know it. It is over. Something is over.

So you think you'll be better in Spanish, you ask. Buenos Aires is my city, isn't it, I mutter in response, far from you on the other side of the kitchen table. That's where the maps seem to lead, but have you not noticed the lack of directional signs, do you think it coincidence that we always return to the same point no matter where we are living—or leaving? Our hands resting solidly on the table, holding it down, preventing it from drifting upwards, or away. The waves coming and falling more frequently now—this voice has become yours, after all—one on the heel of the other like children chasing each other around a rubber plant tree. The thing is, you add, if you really want to go back you should move to Poland, try your luck in Warsaw, Lublin—search there for your lost tribe. (*Si te vas a ir, andate a Varsovia, o Lublín, por favor, ¿qué pretendés encontrar en Buenos Aires, especialmente hoy en día?*) Lost, but of a tribe, maybe. Is it possible, does it make any sense, to say goodbye in English? Will all of this have been about learning a new language in which (with which?) to say goodbye? Is that what tongues are for, hellos and goodbyes? Is there no better use of language?

* * *

Here we are again, you and I, in the middle. Unsure of how or when we began. This decision to finally move back to San Francisco has brought about unexpected consequences. Listening to tango records I inherited from my parents with a view to the Flat Irons. The Rocky Mountains: a young formation, not unlike the Andes. I remember the madwoman's soliloquy in the song, walking randomly through the neighborhood. Just turn the page back, you say. Although we know it is not that simple, look forward to touching in the dark. Two weeks on pain killers lying on my side: that is when it began, or at least something ended then. How quickly an airplane shifts our perspective: south to north, narratives from elsewhere. Slouched and uncomfortable on the couch, I put off my studies for one more song while you prepare the afternoon coffee. By the time the stories are sifted into papers and essays, it will no longer called exile, and another album side will have ended.

* * *

But that was a long time ago, yesterday, and I can see myself already on an airplane, flying back, regardless of whether such a thing is possible, leaving once again.

* * *

But my question to you now, you ask—settling back in your chair instead of leaning over the table as you usually do—my question to you is if this putting together of pieces and fragments, this sudden insistence on ordering and prioritizing, on linear chronology and Euclidean geography, if all of this is related to a new departure. I have agreed to help you organize these papers and photographs, you say, to select and present the vessel with fissures and all (your empty house, my crowded junk drawer), and as soon as I do you decide to go back, to head south instead of west, to pursue a teaching job in Buenos Aires? So we move on to arrange these notes, it is true, I insist on this as if it were all that mattered, this closing shop so many years after my grandparents stopped working in any shop (tailoring, watchmaking), this searching for patterns in the spin of the roulette wheel, winning numbers flashing overhead as if with hidden meanings. It is true, I wish to do this so that I may walk again in a city that is familiar yet foreign, where streets and avenues cover temporal as well as spatial distances and the shade of the trees on the uneven sidewalks feels like home.

* * *

I will do this because you are leaving, you say, I will do this because you have always been leaving and because you must leave, I will do this.

* * *

Go, you say.

It is fitting, I suppose, that I address you from an airplane, again at 33,000 feet (or 10,000 meters, as the pilot announces now that we are out of U.S. airspace), that I write this last note on a fold-out tray, cramped in coach (especially cramped for such a long flight), trying to write and stay focused, beside me a teenager flying alone, fidgeting in his sleep. You have helped me arrange everything to this point; as soon as I land I will mail this letter back so you can put it where it belongs, in order, alongside the other papers. Any additional changes I leave entirely to you, knowing, as you said, that there are countless ways to read our tales of migration.

It would not have worked, you know it as well as I, perhaps better than I. I could not live entirely in English—the same exact words gaining unexpected meanings when said in the other's tongue, at another time—it would not have worked. I understand that you did not want to come with me, that you could not come with me (What would I do there, who would I be, you asked), but is it not true that you choosing north, just as I choose south, makes this a mutual abandoning, a split leaving, you and I in opposite directions for the first time since we met (you and I in opposite directions ever since we first met?). I understand that you did not want to be so far from your Central California family, I understand not wanting to leave. I understand and I hope that my understanding is enough for me to ask you to understand that, just as you had to stay, I had to leave, I had to leave again, this time, I had to see whether a return was possible.

A return to what, to whom, you asked, and I had no answers then, or now.

You always kept me rooted with your questions. I almost said that you always *keep* me rooted with your questions, as if you were still here, on this plane heading southeast, sitting next to me instead of the slouched kid who sleeps through everything (the crackly announcements on the intercom, the frequent air turbulence, the loud dinner service). Indeed, as I write this letter it feels as if you were, however fleetingly, once again my interlocutor, and while I have you— if I have you—as I imagine, you, you reading this, me, me in your hands one last time, I can only say how surprised I am, surprised that I was ever there at all, surprised that there is no more, that I can invoke the tailor and the watchmaker, the physicist and the teacher but no longer the violinist. That I can refer to the aunts and the *mate* and the *pretzelech*, to the blue guitarist and the madwoman's soliloquy (as long as you are willing to respond), to paths found only in map-poems, to chaparral green as seen through the rolled-down window of your VW Thing, to cobblestone steps in the dream of a *rio-platense* neighborhood in one version and to flitting swallows above the cloister of a Franciscan mission in another, to a ride in a chauffeured Torino running reds through the outskirts of Buenos Aires, to a boat race in the Luxembourg gardens— ¡*merde!*—that I can name these things again, leave you with an extended grocery list (our lives, our memories, our dreams: alas, a list), yes, that I can leave you the words but only the words, for that is all I have to leave… Yes, that is the surprise, in reality, I leave and I leave you the words as if I had run out of narratives—and, without narratives, I have no option but to leave. I leave you the titles of the stories but not the stories themselves, the stories I have lost.

I have failed, there is so much still unsaid, we both know it, something about melodies and our bodies touching in the dark… God knows we tried. And so what is said remains as an effort to say the unsayable, to find a language with which to articulate something beyond any tone that you and I knew, or which we were able to create—deluded by the belief that one can create a new form, speak with another tongue, do anything other than express our inability to say what we want to say. And yet what has to be said always gets said, somehow. Such as: thank you, farewell.

No, that is not right, that cannot possibly be right, and you know it—you would say if you were here—you say, perhaps, as you hold me for the last time. You are right, it would be easier to claim that I am out of stories, it would be easier to negate realizations made while lost amid our own snow flurries, just as I once tried to negate the necessity of a nook (corner seat in the café, propped up in bed with a well-directed night lamp), but I cannot, you would not let me, I know. The stories are not over, you would insist if you were here (you might insist as you read this), they may be repeatedly interrupted but they do not end just like that.

(You liked to do many things and everything you wanted to do I did.)

I dozed off for a bit but not for long, I don't believe. The absence of a timepiece has occasional benefits. I am determined to complete this before landing, as if goodbyes were easier in the air, between hemispheres, drifting blindly on either side of the Equator.

I am not sure what I will do in Argentina, nor where I will live, nor how long I will stay. I could take on private English classes to supplement my small salary from the position at the university, or go work in a newspaper (I wonder if *El mundo* has any openings? Perhaps I will give Renzi a call…). I'll stay at first with my friend Omar, my father's childhood friend, he has a studio near Plaza Italia with a foldout couch where he says that I'm welcome to stay for as long as I need. We'll see. I know many people there, as you know, the relatives I haven't seen in years, the aunts and uncles and cousins. I don't know about the *pretzelech*, but I know I'll get *facturas*. Likewise, I doubt that I can find the inner patio, since I am not even sure where the house is—still no one in the family has been able to help me with this, as no one recognizes the house in the dream from my descriptions, but I will look for it, I will look for it, for if I can locate the house then the move will be permanent. And I am sure that I will find my way around, even if I cannot recall the names of the streets at first, I will know where I am on the map.

As you know, I love both kinds of maps, the ones that delineate political boundaries and the ones that depict natural formations, I love the names of the provinces as well as the shape of the ranges, the curves of the rivers, the green flatness of the pampas and the varying brown heights of the mountains and the blue depths of the seas, lakes and other waterways.

(The kid's real world is the one he's found out about ten years too late: its borders begin and end at his name.)

When I was in the fourth grade I memorized the names and locations of the twenty-three provinces of Argentina. Did I ever tell you that one day I waited until everyone had gone out to the patio for recess, including the teacher, and stayed behind to examine in detail the large topographical map of the Southern Cone hanging at the front of the classroom, between the door and the blackboard. I remember at one point closing my eyes and letting my fingertips slide all over the map, feeling the texture and expanse as I repeated to myself the names of the provinces and the major geological locations, going along without having to look at them, from the Puna in the northwest (an extremely arid meseta, average elevation 3,500 meters) to Tierra del Fuego in the southeast. I remember tracing the outlines of Argentina, letting my fingers guide themselves down the edge of the Cordillera (the tallest stretch of the Andes, a mountain range dating back to the Paleogene, also known as the Tertiary Period). I remember touching the highest points, the tall ridges of the peaks of Ojos del Salado (6880 meters), el Tupungato (6800 meters), el Mercedario

(6770 meters), and the zenith, Aconcagua, in the province of Mendoza (6959 meters). And then down to the Patagonian Andes, south of Lake Aluminé (in Neuquén), with its numerous valleys and the continental ice coverings. And inland from there, the vast evenness of the pampas, the Gran Chaco and Mesopotamia. I knew the entire body of the map by tact.

After all our moves we have come to agree that home requires translation. And so I seek one last translation, inside this plane, my overhead light (on the overnight flight to Buenos Aires) providing a miniature pyramid of illumination, a yellow glare on the pages of this lined college notebook—the final one in the series, I suppose. Outside my small area of light it is black, all I can hear is the steady drone of the engines through the night; everyone, beginning with my neighbor, seems to be sleeping. It is late, it feels late, we are changing latitude and longitude and I do not know what time it is, here or there or anywhere. If only I had one of the timepieces that my grandfather used to fix. I imagine you arriving home from work, taking off your heavy jacket, hat and gloves, heading instinctively toward the kitchen table.

Home requires translation, as you liked to say, but does translation require a home? Is that what we had, is that why I am leaving? (Your father pacing around the perimeter of the old, secluded cloister; my grandmother stitching seams with a precision beyond that which can be measured by differential equations.) And, if so—if home requires translation *and* translation requires a home—is my claim to translation any more legitimate than my claim to a home? Does one create a home by translating? Does one need a home to translate? Is translation sufficient to create a home? Did I need to translate myself for you so you could translate yourself (us) for me? And is leaving (this leaving, this attempt to return) part of translation—of home—or its negation?

I knew this would happen, that as soon as I started asking the questions myself I would get completely lost, that I would miss your questions and your words even before my body had had a chance to start missing your body. What might you say at this point, can you tell me about home and translation? I know, you'd tell me to stop, you'd jump in and tell me to stop, to just listen to the language, is this not your story, you'd say, are you and I not in English, is it not enough to mark the difference and move on, you'd ask. I thought I was moving on, but somehow I'd realize that that's not what you meant. You would quickly point out that I'm doing it again, this time trying to say goodbye in English—to English, after all—in English. As your father once said, you'd say, how many immigrants have to abandon their languages before they can claim America as their home?

I have made do with stories that allude to ghosts in empty houses (footsteps down deserted sidewalks, the promise of voices echoing in the plaza, the taste of hazelnut cake dissolving in a boy's mouth) as I tried to convince myself that I am not the ghost, that we are not the ghosts and that the ghosts are not us, *carajo*, they can't be, no matter what my father says. Is he here, though, you'd ask with a furtive glance from the other side of the table and smile as if to chase him away.

* * *

Xeroxed poems, pens and dictionaries spread out all around me, covering the entire table: the empty chair across from me layers of signs and definitions away: would the timepiece function at all? (Would the shop be open, would someone be there, available to repair it?) Open suitcase in the middle of the living room, mirror reflecting no one on the wall. Must I leave to be unstuck at last?

* * *

This work, what's left of it, the final pieces gathered in these cramped quarters, the part of this work that has become an obsession with organization, a question of chronology, a genealogy of reconstructed memories, this work (here, there, wherever there is or was the table and the coffee, wherever, nowhere), filling up one notebook after another, from the *cuaderno San Martín* to the Thrifty workbooks, turning the pages back and forth (depending on the language, depending on who is speaking) as if they were grains of sand sifting through the funnel of a toy sand clock—something about the interconnectedness of gravity and time, my father would say now; something about children learning about time by holding it in their hands, you would say instead, about the sieve of time—always reading and translating on these pages which are about to go back into the trunk (*el baúl que trajimos de la Argentina; el sobre con las páginas que te mandaré ahora que me vuelvo* [sic]), where I leave them for you—or her—to sort.

    I have to get out, I have to try to get out even if speaking about getting out only extends an inability to get out. (My finger pressing gently on the contours of the map, the warmth of your voice in my ear, the wind stirring the leafs around the rubber plant tree, cows chewing endlessly on a plain shadowed by jutting mountains on the muted screen, the hissing of the espresso machine in the café, of the engines on this airplane.) A body that knows only how to face southeast.

    I have boarded this plane as one who seeks to go through the looking-glass, into stories and dreams and memories and promises and shadows and footsteps. I know how this must sound, but my options are limited. I know.

I am out, I cannot believe it, I am finally out. Is this what it feels like to walk on one's own, without debt or political threats, without chronic ailments or doubts about one's direction? Not that one has reached one's destination, but that one knows where one is going, that one knows that the going is ahead and that nothing can stop you from getting there. To walk as if by instinct, not worried about time or deadlines or the names of the streets, to walk for the pleasure of feeling one's legs moving and carrying one's body forward, slight breeze against us, slightly uphill, at a quick and steady pace. Yes, I am out and I am walking and I am walking with you and everything is as it should be.

* * *

I love it here, don't you just love it here?

* * *

The sun high above must be incredibly hot, it always is this time of year, but I don't feel it, walking against the force of the water I am cool and I don't feel the heat or hear anything from outside and I am walking, I can push my legs against the resistance under the surface but I am floating, it is hard work but it is exhilarating, like walking on the moon must be except wet and refreshing, and I know that I must be moving slowly but it doesn't feel that way, for there is no sense of time in here, I am refreshed and I am moving.

* * *

Where are we, can you tell me where we are, please? Is this San Francisco? Yes and no, you say, walking beside me with long, graceful strides. Don't you recognize this? Don't you recognize us? Look around, you say, listen.

* * *

(*Why, my troubled soul, / why languish there in your longing? / Is it leaving your people or household / that holds you back in your grief?*)

* * *

Walking with my child on my shoulders, marching alongside my wife and our compatriots from where we met in front of the Congreso, down Av. de Mayo towards the Plaza before the Casa Rosada where everyone is gathered. It is so crowded it seems as if the entire country has come out, what a great showing, what an extraordinary day. (There is a joke about unstable neutrons that could be made just about now...) I love the weight of my child on my shoulders, light yet solid, I can feel him holding on to my hair with one hand or the other, I can tell that he is looking around, taking it all in from his particular vantage point, I know that he will tell me all about this demonstration one day, tell me what it meant, why we were here.

* * *

Look, there's Lovejoy's Tea Room, you say. But the man and the woman do not stop to go in.

* * *

(Keep them in mind as you go / and your sorrow will find relief...)

* * *

I just left my boy at the shop, the little corner kiosk I've been calling a shop for years now, left him with all those timepieces to fix, they'll have to wait until tomorrow (A clock has plenty of time, hah, hah), the men are waiting for me at the café, the morning is simply not complete if I haven't rolled my dice, had at least two espressos and two vermouths and smoked my filterless cigarettes with my friends, forgetting, at least for a bit, my wife and the kids and the bills and the roaches and the leak in the bathtub that I've been meaning to fix for weeks now. I refuse to even look at my pocket watch today, I just want to walk, walk down Malabia, feel alive and lost in the crowds (*como una gota de lluvia en el río más ancho del mundo*) until I reach the café.

* * *

Would it feel very different to walk in another city, one wonders, in Rio, in London, in New York? How far could one walk, in a city, before having to turn back?

* * *

(For the Lord's shadow is with you, / whether you leave or stay—)

* * *

If you cannot see it, you say, just hold my hand and listen, listen to the words, guess the language. And remember that we are out now, moving, together. Unstuck.

* * *

Pushing the cart down a dusty street, calling out my wares, I let everyone know that the peddler is on their block, that they can come down and get their goods, the peddler with his cart is open for business. Here they are, the notions, the odds and ends, the stretched fabrics, the buttons, pins and needles, cords, strings and shoelaces, small baskets, different kinds of paper and the prize of it all: three books from Warsaw. Pushing this cart is so much better than before, when I used to be a pack-carrier, carried forty to fifty kilos or more on my back all day long (At least it felt that heavy), always dreaming of a cart and now I have one, now I have this one-wheel cart to push in front of me (I even have a stock of broken watches in a small trunk), that's why I know that my dream to be an apprentice will be realized soon, that I'll be able to sell my cart and all my trinkets and become an apprentice in a shop and that soon after that, once the apprenticeship is completed, that I'll have my own profession, that I'll be a tailor and have my own shop one day, no more of this yelling out what I have to offer. Yes, soon, one day, clients will come to me, I'll be able to ask whatever price I want and they'll pay because I'll be the best, I'll be the best and the only tailor worth going to in the Jewish quarter of Lublin—until I leave this old country, that is, and take myself and my skills somewhere where one can really do something with one's life.

* * *

(*And I'll be considered a stranger...*)

* * *

I know that we've talked about this before, the man says to the woman walking beside him. It is late afternoon, that hour just before the fog droops over Twin Peaks and into Noe Valley. They walk at a good pace on the sidewalk of the busiest street in the neighborhood, moving fast enough so that they have to maneuver around the other pedestrians strolling along. The man looks from side to side at the many shops and restaurants that they pass along the way, but although he recognizes them when he reads their names on the signs or awnings—or when he takes a quick glance into the store, at which point they look extremely familiar (Have I been here before, he wonders; have I lived here before?)—the moment that they are past that particular storefront, he can no longer remember its name, or whether he had really seen it prior to this walk (What was that narrow kiosk with the international newspapers and the photography magazines? Or that flower shop with the bouquets displayed on the sidewalk? Was it on this street that we saw the jewelry shop with the kind of earrings that you like? What was that shoe store with the designer manikins on the other side of the window?).

I know that we've talked about this before, the man says again, but should we have a baby soon?

* * *

Don't you think we should get married first, you reply.

Yes, of course, we'll get married and then we'll have a baby soon?

* * *

They have crossed Castro and the climb is much steeper now, they are working against gravity and the cold wind blowing down the side of the hill, leading with their faces. The man tries to remember what they just saw on the block before but he cannot, and soon he starts to look at everything around him (What's that café over there, with the patio and the gardenias, that looks so familiar?), at the various storefronts on the block they are currently on (Oh, there's the sushi restaurant) with a doubly strange sensation: first, because he recognizes the places but does not know from where; and second, because he has become aware that not only will he not recall from where he recognizes them, but that soon, just a few steps away, he will forget what he is registering this time around as well.

* * *

And in this state I continue to walk, working to keep up with the wind and the hill and with you.

* * *

The man and woman walking along, having this conversation after work, before dinner, do not really disagree on the topic of marriage. Neither is that crazy about the institution; you mainly ask because the proposed chronology seems off: should marriage not come before children? What is he asking for, anyway, you wonder. She is not so sure that this distinction, the order of events, really matters that much, but she feels it is her job to clarify such issues, she has always been the one to organize timelines, although he is the one obsessed with questions of reversibility. Her lists, his series.

* * *

And in this state I begin to listen.

* * *

But do not say that all I care about is the making the babies part, either, he says.

 I know, you reply, I know. We both like that part just fine, I won't let you get away with claiming that you like it more than I. And she doesn't.

 So…

 A little girl would be nice, the woman finally says under her breath. (Unusual that she should mutter in this manner.) And then once again, this time with a loud clarity revealing finality and determination: Yes, a little girl would be very nice. Very nice indeed.

* * *

I have circled the steamship so many times that I have lost count. One feels so trapped on a boat, I just had no idea it would be this way. Three months may not seem like much in a person's entire lifetime, one might think of it as barely a short aside in a bulky novel, but when one is living it—when one is confined like this for three full months, crossing the Atlantic, never seeing anything other than blues and grays, ocean and sky, the same long faces over and over again, everyone's complexion pallid and grayish beginning on the second day of travel, when one is out here like a fool—then three months is a veritable eternity. And so I circle the ship along the starboard, head fore until I reach the prow and look out as far as the horizon, always an infinity away. I walk aft along the portside, never too interested in the activities on either leeside, until I reach the stern of the S.S. Almanzora, from where I watch the steam stretching behind the ship, the only evidence that we are actually moving, ever so slowly approaching the end of the parenthesis, enough is enough, I am ready to rejoin the rest of the prose, on land somewhere, take me to a city, any city, on any continent.

* * *

(... *until my bones are worn away.*)

* * *

Can you tell me what has happened? Where are we? Is this San Francisco? Did we move from Boulder? Did I drive a U-haul on I 80 again? How did we get here, you and I?

* * *

Feel the breeze in your hair, just above the line of splashing water.
And in this state he walks along, certain and uncertain of everything.

* * *

And now I know that I can leave this. As if this had been anything other than living. (There is always so much reading to do; so much reading, thank God.) Yes, I will go now, we will go now, there is much to do. For example: practice conjugations, write letters. Thank you. Farewell.